SLATE RUN ANNUAL

VOL. I

Edited by:

James J. Slattery

Published by Slate Run Publishing, LLC.
www.slaterunpublishing.com

Cover design : Slate Run Publishing, LLC
Cover painting : Dayna Winters
Edited by : James J. Slattery

ISBN: 0692327371
ISBN-13: 978-0692327371

DEDICATION

For the mute, inglorious Miltons out there....

Editor's Notes

A collection of stories as disparate as this one might seem to be the product of an editor with no unifying vision. Such, however, is not the case. Each of these stories has been chosen carefully. The primary criterion for selection is artistic merit. The second, and essential element, is that each piece has been written by an author from the greater Capital District. Beyond that, readability, depth of characterization, thematic structure, and timeliness all come into play. Some, like *Mercury Shining*, *The Reckoning*, and *Sweet Dreamz* are SciFi/Fantasy. Some are coming of age as are *The Farthest West Beach* and *The Art of Growing Pains*. Others are directly related to the experiences of soldiers both at war e.g. *Tap Shoes*, and on the battlefields experienced by the veteran upon return such as *Them*. Both of the preceding were written by Ryan Smithson, a veteran of the Iraq War. Others deal with psychological crises particularly *The Boy with a Thousand Arms* and *The Short Plank Jig*.

One of the objects of this publication is to present to the reading public a glimpse into the talent centered within this relatively obscure neighborhood, a mere one hundred and fifty miles from New York City. The mission statement of Slate Run Publication centers itself upon the tragedy of overlooked excellence, Thomas Gray's "Mute inglorious Miltons." We are dedicated to bringing other voices to the artistic smorgasbord. No one represented here is elite. Neither are any of them mute. Some just may be glorious.

The voices of these authors ring with the truth of artistic integrity and very human insights. Most of all, they are alive and writing.

By way of disclaimer I must acknowledge that three of the included works are my own, two as James Slattery — *Days of Wine and Roaches* and *Embarkation*, as well as one, *Another Girl* by JS McInroy, my pseudonym. In order to assure a fair selection process, these were reviewed by an independent editor who found them worthy of inclusion.

[2] Stephen Slattery is my brother. Selection of his work was also delegated to another editor.

Table of Contents

"More Like Me Than Myself" might accurately be classified as a coming of age story. The protagonist, Miranda, most decidedly is thrust into the maelstrom of conflicting hopes, desires, fears, and unwelcome ambiguities so characteristic of that genre. However, to so categorize the story ignores the underlying themes of ethnicity —Italian/American—a particularly American Roman Catholic world view, but most of all, a young girl's awakening not merely into adulthood or gender awareness, but most poignantly into an awareness of self which transcends all labels, all analysis. Miranda comes alive in these few pages, and Miranda is more than the sum of all her facticities. She is developing. But, one is led to assume, will never "come of age." She is, however "becoming," in all its Existential complexity.

More Like Me Than Myself

Maria Palmara

"St. Rita's?" Miranda choked on the words as she swallowed the last bite of her cream cheese and jelly sandwich. "I'm not going to Catholic school," she said. The twelve-year-old licked her fingers and stared at Grandma Zambota and her mother, Kit. For the past three weeks, after watching the morning news, Kit would call into her daughter's bedroom and tell her that she didn't have to get ready for school because the teachers' strike was still on. Miranda had gotten used to the morning routine and figured that the few remaining spring months of the school year would simply turn into a carefree summer spent riding her bike aimlessly through the streets.

"You should be grateful Grandma got you in," her mother said, wiping away sticky breakfast crumbs from the pink Formica table. "You're missing too much school."

"You should thanks God," Grandma Zambota added in her thick Italian accent, which got thicker depending on the situation.

Throughout the spring of 1968, there had been rumors of a public school strike, and many parents had managed to transfer their children to local Catholic schools. Even Ann, her best friend at P.S. 212, had already left their seventh grade class for St. Michael's across town.

Miranda never worried because she knew that her parents couldn't afford to send her to a private school. But that morning Grandma Zambota came to tell them that all her years of

4

volunteering at the church had finally paid off and that she managed to get Miranda into St. Rita's for as long as the strike lasted.

"But I don't want to go," Miranda said. The florescent kitchen light buzzed above her, and she felt her stomach begin to ache.

"What kind of girl doesn't want to go to God's school?" Grandma Zambota's question was aimed at her daughter.

"She'll go, Ma," Kit said, turning from the stove and carefully handing her mother a petite cup and saucer.

"See what happens when you don't go to church," the old woman said, taking the cup into her shaky hand and placing it on the table. "Now look what you get."

"She's going. Don't worry," Kit said, opening a tin of cookies and sliding it across the table. The old woman picked one out, examined both sides, then put it back.

"What's the matter with the St. Rita's school?" Grandma Zambota now sounded hurt. "St. Rita. The saint of the impossible case," she said, as if anybody with half a brain would know that. "What could be better?"

The old woman was a walking hagiography when it came to the lives of saints and was especially proud of her collection of plaster statuettes. The Infant of Prague guarded the kitchen. Saint Anne blessed Kit's old bedroom. Three Virgin Marys stood in a lineup on the old woman's dresser. And perched on top of the tall chest of drawers was the prized statue of Saint Rita, clutching her basket of red fruit and blue flowers.

"She was an Italian girl, you know," Grandma Zambota said, as if that alone raised her to sainthood. "Good to her parents when they got old. Sacrificed herself for her family," she added and then downed her espresso in one shot.

Kit took the cup and saucer and put it in the sink. "It's getting late."

Grandma Zambota gave Kit her *What's the rush about?* face,

reopened the tin, and picked through the cookies some more.

"Daddy said as long as there's a strike I could stay home and help you cook," Miranda said, hoping that playing the "help around the house" card would help.

"Forget it," her mother said.

"But it's all the way up by Grandma's." Miranda heard herself whining.

"You can walk it," her mother said, closing the cookie tin and placing it on top of the refrigerator.

"But the strike might end," Miranda said, and thought about the public school and how she missed her teacher, Miss Marion. In class, Miranda used to pretend that she was having trouble with math problems, so when Miss Marion finally got to her desk, she'd stay a little longer. Once, Miranda arrived early to school, so she could secretly place a rose she picked from her mother's garden on the teacher's desk. It was that night Miranda had the strange dream. In it, Miss Marion was kissing her. The dream had stayed with Miranda all the next day and made her feel good and bad at once.

"If the strike ends," her mother said, pulling her daughter back from her thoughts, "you can go back and finish at 212. But for now, it's St. Rita's."

After Grandma Zambota watched Kit wipe off the area of the table directly in front of her for the second time, the old woman announced that she had to go home. "I've got to start the stracciatella for your father," she said, as if making soup was a punishment. She slowly pulled herself up out of the chair, supporting herself on her rickety metal shopping cart. The old woman wheeled the rusted contraption everywhere. As usual, the wheels were sticking and squeaking as she maneuvered it through the kitchen. At a particularly high-pitched screech, Miranda covered her ears and felt the hairs on her arms stand straight up.

"Get Pop to oil that thing for you," Kit said.

Grandma Zambota sighed and lightly kicked one of the wheels with her small black shoe. "I'm always the last one he remembers," she said, as she slipped on her black coat and tied her kerchief snugly under her chin. "Oh, I almost forgot!" The old woman perked up as she pulled a crumpled shopping bag out of the cart. "Look," she said as she wiggled out the contents. "A St. Rita's uniform from the church basement…free!" She carefully unfolded the faded plaid jumper and matching navy blazer that had an image of St. Rita herself embossed on the lapel.

"It smells," Miranda complained as her mother held the jumper against her.

"We'll wash it."

"It's too big."

"It's fine."

"Can't we shorten it?" Miranda said, looking down the long skirt.

"No!" Grandma Zambota quickly cut in. "We have to give it back."

THE FOLLOWING MORNING, Miranda and her mother were sitting on the hard wooden bench outside the admissions office of St. Rita's. She had on the old school uniform, which had been loosely tacked to fit her. Her long brown hair was braided tightly and was pinching the back of her neck. On the wall across from where they sat hung a giant oil painting entitled "*St. Rita of Cascia*" and under it a golden plaque read, "*Please let me suffer like you, Divine Savior.*"

Miranda snapped her book strap as she studied the painting. In it, St. Rita was wearing a grey habit and kneeling in front of a small wooden altar. Above the altar hung a large crucifix with a long, slim Jesus nailed onto it. The saint gazed directly into her Savior's eyes, her mouth slightly opened, a hand reaching out to Him. It seemed to Miranda that the saint had been asking for something, maybe a favor, but had been cut short in mid-sentence by a dead-white laser beam that was shooting from the head of Christ and boring a hole directly in the center of the woman's forehead. It reminded Miranda of a Godzilla movie she had once seen, the one where the monster destroys an entire Japanese city with deadly rays from his eyes. But here, in the painting, the beam didn't seem to bother St. Rita. In fact, she looked happy, even though the laser packed such a punch that it knocked the figs and flowers right out of her basket and onto the floor.

After a few minutes, the large door to the admissions office finally swung open. "Mrs. Varia?" A short, elderly nun in a black habit appeared. "Come in," she said, as she ushered them in and directed them to sit in the two small chairs that were placed in front of her immense wooden desk. Sister Francis Henry introduced herself, shook Kit's hand once, and nodded in Miranda's direction.

"I have good news," she began, as she swiveled into her chair and slipped on a pair of rimless glasses. "We arranged temporary placement for your daughter. But with the strike, the seventh grade is completely full. We have room in the sixth. But I am sure that will be challenging enough for your daughter." As she spoke, her stiff wimple cut into her pink fleshy face. "We're always ahead of the public schools," she assured Kit. "Believe me," she said, looking over the top of her glasses. "Your daughter would be challenged in the fifth grade here."

Miranda squirmed in her seat and began to snap her book strap again. Her mother shot her a look, and she stopped.

Kit turned back to the old nun. "What about the eighth?" she asked. "Is there room there?" Miranda couldn't believe her mother had asked such a thing and listened as she went on to describe her stellar report cards. "And as you said, it's only temporary. It will give her a head start on next year."

Miranda twisted her book strap around her fingers as she

waited for the old nun to respond.

"Well… yes," Sister Francis Henry slowly answered, glancing at her watch. "There's more room in the eighth. It's true. And frankly, it makes little difference to me. This strike has caused us enough disruption. But if she falls behind, she'll have to go back."

The old nun signaled that the conversation was over by closing a notebook that seemed to have nothing to do with their meeting. "I'll meet you outside," she said, nodding to the door. Kit thanked her, and she and Miranda quietly stepped out into the hall.

Miranda looked up at her mother. "Eighth grade?"

"You'll be fine," Kit said, as she straightened Miranda's collar and brushed off her faded blazer. "You'd be there soon enough anyway."

Sister Francis Henry came out of the office and shook Kit's hand again. "All right," she said, "I'll take her down to the class now."

Kit adjusted her daughter's collar once more, kissed her on the forehead, and left her in the charge of the old nun. Miranda followed Sister Francis Henry down the hall, trailing behind the woman's flowing black robes and shining black shoes until they finally stopped outside one of the classrooms. The old nun opened the door without knocking and gestured to the young nun teaching the class to come to the door. Miranda was introduced to Sister Mary Andrew and then told to go in and take a seat. Sister Francis Henry closed the door behind her, so the two nuns could speak in private.

With their teacher gone, the students immediately began whispering among themselves. Miranda walked to the back of the classroom, sat in the last row, and looked around the room. It looked a lot like 212, except for the large crucifix on the wall above the teacher's desk.

She scanned the room to see if she recognized anyone and noticed a boy named Frankie who was at a party at Ann's a few months earlier. Miranda had never been to a party like that before. It had been in the basement, and Ann's parents had stayed upstairs. The latest Beatles' 45s were blasting, and there was real Coca-cola and onion dip. At one point, Ann announced that they were all going to play a game. She paired each boy up with a girl, and Frankie got Miranda. When Ann turned out the lights, Frankie immediately pulled Miranda to him. The quick hot breath in her ear, and the damp sticky lips against her neck shocked her. But Miranda found herself turning to face the boy anyway. Before anything could happen, Ann's mother opened the basement door and turned the lights back on and said to keep them on. For weeks after, Miranda wondered what it would have been like to have actually kissed the boy.

Miranda snapped her book strap as she continued to scan the classroom. In the opposite back corner, she saw someone else she knew. At the beginning of last summer, Miranda heard Grandma Zambota telling her mother that her neighbor, old Mr. Spellini, had died and that his son was moving his whole family into the house to take care of his widowed mother.

Later that week, Miranda rode her bike to the Spellini house hoping to see the new neighbors. A tall, skinny boy wearing a baseball cap, a grey sweatshirt, and jeans was in front of the house randomly swinging a bat at some tall weeds. Miranda rode by to get a closer look, but the brim of his cap was pulled down, covering most of his face.

When she reached the end of the block, she turned the bike around and rode by again. This time, he stopped swinging and looked up at her. Miranda could see the large blue eyes and delicate features that had been hidden under the cap. And she saw the thick ponytail that had been stuffed down the back of the sweatshirt. The new boy was a girl. Miranda didn't stop to talk to her as she might have with other new girls. Instead, she pedaled even faster, almost falling over on the turn to her grandmother's block.

In the classroom, Miranda barely recognized the odd girl disguised by the school uniform. Her black, kinky hair was pinned down by two wide barrettes and pulled back in a thick rubber band. Her knees scraped the bottom of her desk. Even from across the room, Miranda could see the girl's coarse leg hair crushed under her stockings. She looked down at her own black tights and regretted that the nylons were the one part of the required uniform for girls in the eighth grade at St. Rita's that her mother wouldn't allow.

The odd girl noticed that Miranda had been staring and looked back at her. Her flattened hair framed her pale face making her blue eyes seem even more intense than Miranda remembered. She nodded toward Miranda as if she knew her, but looked away when Sister Mary Andrew finally returned to class.

While the teacher took attendance, Miranda listened carefully for the strange girl's name. "Christina?" she called. The girl looked up, and raised a hand, then opened a book and read.

The girl disturbed Miranda. *Why did she look at me like she knew who I was?*

FOR THE FIRST few days at St. Rita's, Miranda sat alone during lunch and stood by herself at recess. Even Frankie didn't talk to her. Miranda knew that the reason she was being ignored was because she was from public school. Christina was also always alone. But Miranda felt that Christina Spellini was outcast for some other reason, so she, too, kept her distance.

Aside from her failing social life, the schoolwork at St. Rita's was a lot harder than Miranda imagined. The pages and pages of homework were difficult, and she quickly fell behind in everything, especially math. By the end of her first week, Sister Mary Andrew appeared satisfied when she handed Miranda her second failing quiz grade. Not long after, the young nun sent home a note saying that if Miranda didn't improve soon, she would have to go to the sixth grade as was originally suggested.

That afternoon, Miranda came home and changed out of her uniform into shorts and a tee shirt. The note was folded on the kitchen counter between them as the girl sat at the table, watching her mother make dinner.

"Well, you gave it a try," Kit said, as she mixed the bowl of chopped meat and eggs together with one hand. "The sixth won't be so bad. It's only temporary anyway."

Miranda didn't answer. She could feel her legs sticking to the vinyl as she fidgeted in the chair. *There is no way I'm going back to the sixth*, she thought.

"Throw that in," her mother said, nodding to a small pile of parsley on the table.

The girl took the plate and as she slid the green leaves into the bowl, the familiar high-pitched screech could be heard coming up their walkway. "Grandma's here," she said, rubbing the hairs on her arms back down.

As the front door opened, Kit looked at her daughter and sighed.

"I came as soon as I heard the news," Grandma Zambota shouted over her shoulder as she backed her creaky metal shopping cart into the kitchen.

"What news?" Kit asked, wiping off her hands.

"About Miranda failing school!" The grandmother spoke as if she were talking to idiots.

"How did you hear?" Kit questioned her mother suspiciously.

"Well, it's not because anyone here ever tells me anything," she said, taking off her coat and untying her kerchief. She walked over to the sink and as she rinsed her hands, Grandma Zambota explained that at the church rummage sale that very morning she had simply mentioned in passing how clever it was of Miranda to have skipped a full grade when entering St. Rita's. "And then I have to hear from Sister Catherine that Miranda's falling behind!"

The old woman stopped to catch her breath and slip on an apron. "So I right away go to see Millie Spellini from around the corner," she said, pointing a wet finger in the air to emphasize the greatness of her idea. "You know her granddaughter's in Miranda's class. We made a plan for the two girls to study together. " Grandma Zambota gave Kit her *I was only trying to help* face as she dried her hands. "It won't look good if she's put back," she said.

Miranda turned to her mother. "I'm not studying with her," she said, struggling to form the hunk of meat she had taken out of the bowl.

"Why not? Millie says Christina's a smart girl. She's new at St. Rita's, too." The grandmother took the meat out of Miranda's hands, threw half back, and quickly rolled the remainder into a ball. "What's the problem? She'll show you what's what," she said holding a meatball up to Miranda as if displaying a rare jewel. "If you make them smaller," she said, her brown eyes twinkling, "you get more."

"We can do these, Ma," Kit said, moving the bowl away from her mother.

Grandma Zambota walked over to the stove, picked up the wooden spoon, and began stirring the sauce. "You didn't use puree, did you?" she asked. "It gives me the agita."

Kit pretended not to hear. "Well," she said to Miranda, placing a huge meatball on the pan, "you can try working with this girl, or you can go into the sixth for a while. It's up to you."

THE NEXT DAY after school, Miranda rode her bike up to the Spellini house. As she approached, she saw old Mrs. Spellini bent over picking weeds from the lawn. Beyond her, she saw Christina, who had already changed into her sweatshirt and jeans. She was playing ball with her father and younger brother. Christina had just hit the ball and was running to the rose bush that served as a base. Her brother grabbed the ball and quickly threw it to his father, who caught it, then grabbed his daughter around her waist, lifted her off the ground, and began tickling her unmercifully. "Stop!" she screamed, laughing and struggling to get away. The boy jumped onto their father's back and all three fell over onto the grass and continued wrestling.

"All right, that's enough," Christina's mother called to them through the screen door. "It's time for Christina to come in."

"Why? Is it time to eat already?" her father said, holding both his children tightly under his arms.

"Joe…" The woman tilted her head and sounded annoyed. "You're being too rough with her again."

"We're only playing," her father laughed, setting his children free.

"You know," she said, lowering her voice "We talked about this…" She stopped when she noticed Miranda standing quietly next to her bike. "Look," she said, "Christina's friend's here now anyway. This is Angie Zambota's granddaughter, Miranda. They're going to do homework together."

"Ok, honey," her father said to Christina, "I guess you have to go in."

Christina picked up her baseball cap that had fallen off and pulled it over her long, kinky hair, which was in still in a ponytail, but stuffed down the back of her sweatshirt.

"Alright," she said, not looking directly at Miranda. "Let's go inside."

As the two girls passed, old Mrs. Spellini held up a bunch of dandelion greens she had just picked off the lawn. "These you stew up in red sauce," she said to Miranda. "Next time you come, I'll show you girls how to cook them."

Next time? Miranda thought. *I'm just here for today.*

Miranda followed Christina into the house and to her bedroom, which was large and seemed to be painted pink. It was hard to tell because the walls were covered with posters of baseball players and racing cars. The shelves were filled with books, but there were also softballs, baseball cards, and model cars everywhere. In one corner sat a wooden box filled with faded stuffed animals, disheveled baby dolls, and a few twisted Barbies. On top was a large bride doll sitting lopsided, her long bare legs poked out the side of her white crinoline petticoat. Christina removed a catcher's mitt from her desk so that Miranda could work there and spread out her own books on her bed.

"Nice room," Miranda said.

"It's okay," Christina said, not looking up from her math book. "If you need help, just ask."

Miranda opened her book and sat staring at the unfamiliar symbols, but could not bring herself to ask the strange girl for help. Instead, she began reading all the framed certificates of achievement hanging on the wall above the desk. Not only was Christina good in math, but she also received awards for writing, science, and history.

As Miranda read the certificates, she noticed that in the center of them all hung a small version of the curious painting of St. Rita. She thought of what Sister Mary Andrew had said the day their class walked by the large painting when they were on their way to assembly. The young nun stopped to explain that what Christ was doing in the scene was sending St. Rita one of the thorns from his crown and lodging it into her head to show that he loved her. She told them the thorn gave the woman head trouble the rest of her earthly life, but it was a sure sign that she was saint material. "A genuine martyr," she said. *Why would anyone want that?* Miranda had wondered. *It must've really hurt.*

"What's the matter?" Christina asked, pulling Miranda back into the room.

"Nothing," she said, embarrassed that she was caught reading the certificates, "I couldn't find the page," she said, and returned

15

to her book and listened to Christina scratch out answers with her pencil. *Great*, Miranda thought. *She must be way ahead by now.*

As Miranda stared at the problems, she heard the squeaking wheels of her grandmother's shopping cart through the opened window. *I can't believe she followed me here*, she thought as she listened to Grandma Zambota and old Mrs. Spellini speaking the Italian dialect and cackling like ancient hens.

"Do you want me to show you how to do these?" Christina asked, finally noticing that Miranda was not writing. "It's really not that hard."

Christina got up and leaned over Miranda and began explaining the steps. As Miranda listened, she could feel the girl's warmth next to her. A soft scent pulled her mind from one concentration to another. Then, she noticed the small vase of blue flowers next to the girl's bed.

"Are you listening?" Christina asked. Her large blue eyes stared at Miranda from across the desk.

"Yeah," Miranda nodded, and forced herself to focus on the homework.

Christina watched as Miranda tried to work out a problem on her own. "I've seen you around here," she said after a few minutes, "on your bike."

"Yeah, I ride up here a lot. My grandparents live around here." Miranda felt a small rush of shame for ignoring Christina whenever she rode by.

"Do you like St. Rita's?"

"No. I hate it." The anger in her voice surprised her. "I can't wait for the strike to end."

"It's hard when you don't know anyone."

"I know Frankie Ramone," she said, not wanting the odd girl's sympathy. "We made out."

Christina didn't respond. She just took the pencil from Miranda and checked over the homework.

"How are you girls doing?" Christina's mother startled them both as she entered the room. She immediately walked over to the toy box and retrieved the bride doll. "I keep telling you you're going to ruin this," she said, fluffing the white gown. Christina watched her mother return the delicate creature to its rightful place in the center of the bed. "Are you two almost done?"

"We're done," Christina said and closed Miranda's book.

"Good. We're going to eat soon," her mother said, adjusting the doll's veil before leaving.

Miranda packed up her books, and Christina walked her to the front door.

"I'll walk you home," she said.

"I got my bike."

"I'll walk you half way."

When they got outside, Miranda looked around for Grandma Zambota, who was nowhere in sight. The two girls walked in silence as Miranda awkwardly wheeled her bike between them.

"It's a hard place to get to know people," Christina finally said. "St. Rita's, I mean."

"I don't care about meeting people at St. Rita's. It's only temporary for me." Miranda said, knowing that her remark would somehow hurt the girl. Christina slipped her hands into her pockets of her jeans and looked down at the sidewalk as they continued. They finally passed what Miranda figured to be the halfway mark between their houses. "Okay," she said, and got on her bike. "Thanks for the help."

"We can do this tomorrow if you want," Christina said.

"Let's see what the homework is first." Miranda positioned herself to pedal away.

"Wait a minute. I want to show you something. Wait here."

Miranda watched as Christina ran across the street and down a hill into an empty wooded area. The neighborhood was filled with sunken lots ever since the city raised the streets for the new water system. These days, most people use them as dumps, places to throw away old baby carriages, bald tires, broken appliances, and other junk. When they were younger, she and Ann used to go down into them searching for treasure. One summer, they found a pair of ice skates and took turns wearing them all day. She missed Ann and wondered when she'd ever see her again.

Christina finally reappeared holding a handful of blue flowers. Miranda was fascinated by their unusual color, then realized they were the same as those in the vase next to the girl's bed. "I've never seen ones like these before," she said.

"Yeah, I know. The only place I've ever seen them is back there," Christina said, nodding to the lot. "Here, take them."

Miranda hesitated, but then looked at the rich color and decided they were too beautiful to turn down. She took the small bunch and put them on top of her books in the basket on her handlebars. "Thanks" she said, "I really have to go now."

As Miranda pedaled home, the wild blue flowers vibrated in the wire basket. *When 212 opens*, she thought as she watched them, *I'll go back and pick some for Miss Marion.*

When she finally walked in the door, Miranda found her mother kneeling on their red and white checkered floor reorganizing the cabinet under the kitchen sink.

"Go get washed," she said, turning and looking over her shoulder. "Daddy's already home. We're going to eat in a little while." But before Miranda could get out of the kitchen, her mother stopped her. "Where'd you get those?" she asked, looking at the flowers in her daughter's hand.

"I picked them myself from a lot I passed."

"They're pretty," she said. "Put them in a glass of water." Miranda did as she was told, and Kit returned to the business of the cabinet.

THE NEXT DAY at St. Rita's, Miranda produced the correct

answers in math during the homework review. When Sister Mary Andrew commented on her miraculous improvement, Miranda was careful not to glance in Christina's direction.

Math was only getting harder, so Miranda's tutoring sessions continued. The two studied every day after school in Christina's room. And afterward, Christina would walk Miranda home, half way. By the end of the second week, Miranda's quiz grades improved enough so that there was no more talk of moving to a lower grade.

During the day, Miranda didn't have it in her to ignore Christina as the others were since she was the one keeping her from being sent back a grade. So she sat with her during lunch, stood near her at recess, and walked home with her.

Not only do they hate me because I am from the public school, she thought, *but now they think I am friends with her.* Miranda felt bad for thinking of Christina that way, but she knew that there was something different about the girl, and their friendship was not helping her meet others at St. Rita's.

During a lunch break one day, Miranda noticed that Frankie and a few other boys were in the schoolyard playing stickball. Christina had gone to the library to return a book, so Miranda decided to go watch the game. She had been trying to get Frankie to notice her ever since she started going to St. Rita's. *After all,* she thought, *we practically kissed.*

As soon as Miranda stepped outside, she noticed a group of girls from her class standing near the chain link fence on the other side of the schoolyard. One of the girls leaned over and whispered in her friend's ear, and they started laughing. Miranda knew they were talking about her, but she continued to inch closer to the game anyway. Frankie was standing in the middle of the field with his back to her as Miranda moved behind him.

"Get out of the way," the boy at bat shouted before he lightly tossed the small rubber ball in the air in front of him, swung, and hit it high overhead. Miranda stood watching the ball, which seemed to be flying directly toward her. As Frankie ran backwards following the ball with his hands overhead, he accidentally knocked into Miranda, and they both fell to the ground.

"Keep out of the way," he said, getting up and brushing off his pants.

"Pervert," the boy at first base called in her direction.

Miranda picked herself up and saw that the loosely tacked hem of her jumper had ripped, leaving it hanging unevenly.

"Where'd you get that uniform?" one of the girls from across the field shouted, "The dump?"

"Oh, look…" Frankie called to the others when he saw that Christina had come out into the schoolyard. "Her girlfriend's coming to save her!"

"Stop it, Frankie," Christina said, as she walked toward Miranda.

"Mind your own business, Brillo head," he said, and looked to his friends to laugh at his joke.

"I mean it," Christina said, walking up to him.

Frankie turned to his friends again. "Oooo…she means it!" he said. "I'm so scared…" Before he could finish his sentence, Christina pushed the boy so hard that he lost his balance and tripped over backwards.

"Stupid lezzie," he said, leaning up on one arm and wiping the dirt streaks off the side of his pants.

"You better watch out, Frankie," another one of the girls from the group yelled across to him. "The dyke's gonna get you."

As Christina turned toward the girls, Frankie sat up and pitched the small rubber ball that he had been holding in his hand directly at Christina. The girl doubled over, and held both hands over her forehead. Miranda moved to help her, but before she could, Christina straightened up and, as if transformed by the blow, ran toward Frankie, and threw herself on top of him.

"Get off me, freak!" he yelled, as he struggled to push her off.

Christina held his arms down with her weight and began beating his head with her fists. The others quickly gathered around to watch. Miranda tried to pull Christina off the boy, who continued to yell for the wild girl to stop.

Within minutes, Sister Francis Henry appeared, swooping down upon the three like a giant nocturnal creature. She seized both Christina and Frankie by the back of their shirts with such force that Miranda was knocked onto the ground again.

"What is the matter with you two?" The old nun shouted as she shook Christina with one hand, and then released Frankie and slapped him hard on the back of his head. The boy backed away from her and looked down, but Miranda could see the blood and tears on his face.

After Sister Francis Henry had gathered up all the offenders and cleared the schoolyard, she turned Frankie and two other boys over to Father St. Jim, who had also arrived on the scene and always handled the boys when it came to discipline.

The old nun led Miranda and Christina to her office and seated the two on the hard wooden bench across from the giant painting of St. Rita. "It's time to stop this nonsense and start acting your age," she said. "Especially you, Spellini. You need to straighten up. Start taking care of yourself. Try doing something with that mop of yours," she said, as she pulled out the remaining barrette dangling from the girl's hair and handed it back to her. "You're a young lady now. Someday you'll be wives...mothers. You need to start thinking about the future," she said.

"Boys are different. They're free." she continued. "Like they're flying on a trapeze." As she spoke, she looked up at the ceiling as if she were watching a circus act. "Girls," she said, returning to the two of them. "They have to be careful. It's not the same for girls. Boys can hurt you in ways you don't yet understand." Her last warning had an uncharacteristic tone of concern.

Sister Francis Henry directed the girls to move to opposite ends of the bench. "Sit for a while and think about what you've done," she said and then glanced up at the looming portrait. "Ask St. Rita for guidance," she added, as if hit with an inspirational second thought. "She'll show you what's right." The old nun went back into her office, leaving the door partly opened so that she could keep an eye on the two rebels.

Miranda sat on the hard wooden bench and scrutinized the painting of the stunned woman. If she were going to ask St. Rita for anything right now, it would be to snap out of her trance and end the public school strike. She looked down the bench at Christina, who sat with her hands folded and her eyes shut. The bruise on her forehead was bright red. *She looks so intense*, Miranda thought. *Maybe she's really praying.*

They sat there for the rest of the afternoon. Ten minutes after school let out, Sister Francis Henry allowed the two to go back to the classroom and pick up their books. "You should know that both of your parents have been called," she said to them before they were released.

"This is so unfair," Miranda complained as they walked home. "Why did we get punished? They started it. This would never have happened at 212."

Christina stopped walking and turned to Miranda. "I can't go home yet," she said. "Not like this."

Miranda looked at the girl's swollen forehead, ripped nylons, and torn shirt. "Maybe we could do something with your hair," she said, tucking a long, curly strand back behind the girl's ear. "Let's go to that lot where those blue flowers grow," Miranda said, figuring that bringing a few flowers home to her mother after Sister Francis Henry called couldn't hurt. "We can try to fix you up a little down there before you go home."

The two made their way through the streets until they came to

22

the sunken wooded lot. They ran down the dirt path, passing a rusted wringer washer, a stack of ripped window screens, a cracked kitchen sink until finally they came to a small clearing under a large leafy tree.

"It's so beautiful here," Miranda whispered as she surveyed the field of curious blue flowers, so many more than she had imagined. Their soft scent filled Miranda and reminded her of that first afternoon in Christina's bedroom.

"Yeah, they're all in bloom now," Christina said, throwing her books aside and sitting down on the ground. Miranda sat down next to her and began to twist her book strap around her fingers while the two quietly watched the wild flowers sway in the breeze.

"Thanks for helping me today," Miranda finally said, reaching out and running her hand over the tops of a small patch of blue.

Christina turned to Miranda "I don't know what happened," she said, "It's like it wasn't me." As she spoke, Miranda saw that the girl's eyes were the same color as the fiery blue flowers behind her. "I hated it there before you came. And you know what else?" she said, sitting up straighter. "I never pray for the things they tell me to. I never pray to become a good wife or a good mother. I never want to turn into a lady. In fact, I pray every day that I don't." She turned away and looked back into the field of blue.

"I used to ask God to not make things happen to me," she said. "You know...things to my body. But that didn't work. So now I make deals with St. Rita." She reached and pulled a handful of flowers out of the ground. "I ask her to stop making me change. You know what I mean?" She sat back and crushed the flowers in her hand. "If I study really hard. If I always do good on everything," she said, turning to look directly at Miranda again. "Maybe St. Rita will stop all that from happening to me. Because she's the one that you can ask for help when there is no hope."

As Miranda listened, she thought of her own fears about the world waiting for her, one so much like her mother's, but she pushed it from her mind as she always had.

Christina sat back against the tree and peeled the damp blue petals from her palms. Miranda turned to Christina and tucked the curly lock that had again fallen from behind her ear. The bruise on the girl's forehead was now a dark red circle. Miranda gently slid her fingers across it, and as she leaned in closer to examine the damage, Christina leaned toward her. The light brush of Christina's lips against hers surprised her. Miranda pulled away, but then she found herself turning back and pulling Christina closer. The two girls held each other for a moment and then Miranda kissed her.

As they kissed, Miranda became aware of the rapid beating of her own heart below her starched white blouse. Her eyes were closed but now and again, she'd open them to see if it were all really happening. The leafy tree and soft scent of the blue flowers surrounded Miranda and gave her an odd sense of security, as if she were in a cave far away.

Above, the leaves rustled in the breeze, and the late afternoon sun ignited the field around them. As they continued to kiss, Miranda thought she heard the faint chirping of birds in the tree branches overhead…*but maybe it was farther away*, she thought as she began listening more closely…*maybe on the sidewalk above*… a sound she knew. The high-pitched screech from the rusted metal shopping cart directly above made the hairs on her arms stand straight up.

"Miranda?" Grandma Zambota called as if she had never heard her own granddaughter's name before. "I thought that was you I saw running across the street before," she said, moving her head side to side, trying to see down through the leaves and branches. "What are you doing down there?" she said, pulling a branch aside so that she could see.

Miranda pushed Christina away, looked up, and through the shadowy tree above saw Grandma Zambota. The old woman let the branch swing back and then began kicking one of the rusted wheels with her small black shoe until she finally managed to turn the old cart around. As the grandmother hurried away, Miranda saw her kerchief gently slip off her shoulders and fall to the ground.

The two girls sat motionless as they listened to the sound of the screeching wheels fade. Miranda was sure her grandmother was making a beeline to her house.

"I'd better go," Miranda said after a few minutes.

"I'll walk you."

"No. I'll be all right."

Miranda picked up her books and left Christina alone in the clearing under the tree in the middle of the field of blue flowers. She climbed back up the path and when she got to the top, she saw her grandmother's kerchief lying innocently on the sidewalk. She picked it up and shoved it in the pocket of her blazer.

When Miranda got to her house, she saw her grandmother's shopping cart parked outside the front door. *She was in such a hurry to tell*, she thought, *she didn't even bother to drag the old thing in with her.* Miranda walked in the front door and felt her heart pounding even harder than it had been just a little while before. She stopped at the entrance to the kitchen because she could see that her mother had just finished mopping, but Grandma Zambota hadn't noticed and tracked through the wet kitchen floor.

"I was going to call," Grandma Zambota said, leaning on the table trying to catch her breath "but then decided to take a walk over with the paper and tell you myself." The old woman avoided looking at her granddaughter as she spoke.

Her mother leaned the sponge mop against the counter and held up the paper so Miranda could read the headline. "The strike's over!"

"Thanks God!" Grandma Zambota said, as she dragged a chair out from under the table and collapsed into it. "Now, you can go back to your school with your nice little friends." While the old woman spoke, she ran her thin, veined fingers across the top of her coat and then nervously looked around on the floor. "Well, it's a good thing," she said, giving up the search, "I never liked that St. Rita school so much."

"Go get changed now. Daddy will be home soon," her mother said, picking up the mop and running it over her mother's foot prints.

Miranda went up to her room without saying a word. She took off her blazer and threw it in the corner, kicked off her shoes, and fell onto her bed. Soon she'd be back at 212. She'd see Miss Marion and maybe Ann would come back. She turned on her side and looked at the blazer crumpled on the floor. Grandma Zambota's kerchief hung out of the pocket. The gold emblem of St. Rita stared back.

Miranda turned away and closed her eyes, curled up around a pillow, and drifted back to the sunken wooded lot, beyond the shadowy branches, down into the clearing where the honest blue flowers waited and rocked quietly in the new spring breeze.

"The Art of Growing Pains" is a coming of age story about a young girl in Albany, NY. Although the situation and events are purely fictional, the emotional backdrop of the piece itself is based on the author's life — getting to know and find herself in a world of uncertainty and fear.

"The Art of Growing Pains" is told from an omniscient point of view; the main character is unnamed. As the story unfolds, the reader is intimately acquainted with the heartbreaking world of neglect and abuse she experiences living with her drug addicted father.

In the end she will be faced with the choice to endure what she has known all her life, or go at it alone...

The Art of Growing Pains

Katie Burns

The paneled walls of the front parlor seemed to close in on her as she wrote – and she was writing for her life. Threadbare carpeting lined the floor of the too-small room and held all the smells of those who had lived there before her and her father, but now it mostly smelled of urine from their dog Shadow. The windows were tightly shut, and flannel bed sheets mocked drab curtains as they hung collecting dust over the windows.

There wasn't much time now. She knew once he came home he would lock himself in the back room all night, and possibly for days, and so her 14 year old mind found the words to write – because she could not bring herself to say them. She had heard it said once somewhere that *real writer's exact real change*, and if this was at all possible, it was exactly what she intended to do. She would change him.

> *Dear Pop;*
>
> *I'm really scared. Kids in the neighborhood call you names and I don't know if they are true or not but I think they might be. I can never bring my friends home because you don't want anyone in the house – and I don't either since it is so nasty! You never give me any money for school lunch anymore and last week you sent me with a bag of pennies on the school fieldtrip and I couldn't even ride the rides because they didn't accept coins that weren't rolled! Everyone laughed at me. You are always leaving me home alone and because I can't walk Shadow by myself he stays with me inside and pees in the house. We never have enough cat food for Cariboo and he is always whining. Oh- and*

another thing, I hate watching the windows for you when you get all sketchy! No one is going to come in the house Dad. It's so creepy. Also, some of the friends you bring home with you to "party" do things that make me feel uncomfortable. I'm older now and I know it's wrong. I don't want to tell anyone else because I don't want child protective services to take me away again. I hope you understand. I love you. I don't want anything bad to happen. Please stop, for me?

Love, your best friend

It had been going on for a while now – him trying to escape from the world. After the death of his father he had tripped and fallen on grief, and never recovered. Now, long days were spent tethered to the needle and pipe. The obsessive nature of his brain sent him spinning out of control and he was by all standards, possessed.

She licked the edges of the envelope and carefully tucked the letter inside. Standing, she smoothed her pants and rubbed the tears from her eyes. More than sadness, she felt fear.

For a long time now, she had lived in the whirlwind of his chaos and unpredictability. On the days he was able to find work that paid enough for him to score, life was so intoxicating it seemed to get them both high. But nothing was guaranteed, and the days were many that she went without food so that he could get his next one. Often she found herself praying to God for her father to come home high, and it twisted her heart like scrap metal in a junk yard.

On the nights she was left home alone, her stomach churning with anxiety and loneliness, she climbed into bed calling for her cat, (who was just as hungry as she was) to come and fill a void that could never seem to be filled. In all the time she spent alone, she came to know a part of herself that was so desperate, it could only be soothed when she wrote, and so that is what she did.

Every day, she wrote. She wrote songs, she wrote love letters to the boys in school (though she never mailed them), and made up her own quotes with the intention of becoming famous one day. She kept a rigorous journal and recorded everything, though she was careful not to incriminate her father. She had learned her lesson the last time Child Protection nosed around and came across an entry in her diary which was intended to be a formal essay entitled, "Good Touch vs. Bad Touch." The essay had dissected the meaning of bad touch and implied that all of it might not be so bad if it earned you a couple of extra dollars from the older boys at school. And she also wrote poetry.

Come and Go

Color me happy Girl.
Back pack- toting,
"Miss live and let live!"
And
When they're out for blood
Just give
And give
And give.
Listen to the raging silence that your prison brings
And the cocaine violence that your past still sings
Dynamic disaster
In every sense
Perfectly imperfect.
Beautifully Intense.

Aside from her extra-curricular activities that had earned her lunch money and money for pet food, school was her refuge. On the days she wasn't busy fending off insults from the kids who didn't like the jeans she had worn every day that week, and probably the week before, she found comfort in books and the inner quiet they afforded her. Almost always she found herself pretending to be their characters; be it Alice or Charlotte – in a moment, she could be anyone. Anyone but herself.

While she was busy figuring out how to grow up, she grew up. Her body had betrayed her and she had become a woman without fair warning – a little girl grown up in an instant. She pilfered the local drug store monthly for her feminine needs and was almost always eyed suspiciously by the store clerk on her way out the door. Walking home, her pants stuffed with Kotex, she wondered where the people were, who were supposed to be taking care of her.

HE HAD COME into her room shortly after midnight, and because she recognized his face as a friend of her fathers, she wasn't scared – not until he started undressing. She had read in books that the first time would hurt. And it did. Afterwards, she lay still in a small pool of her own blood, with no energy to move from the spot in which she had just shared with a man she'd known all her life – a man who had become a predator in a moment's time. Afterwards, she did not take the fetal position as girls so often do in the movies. She simply lay, floating in and out of a dream-like state, turning the word RAPE over in her mind and spinning it into the incoherent anagram APER, and then gotten up to wash herself clean.

She never told her father what happened. She chose instead to share her secrets through her poetry.

The soul of a child is a delicate thing –
Wound it once and give it wings.

Cry not. For no one will hear.
Endure the pain, despite your fear.

Days flew past. Years crawled by.

The Art of Growing Pains

All the while, war raged inside.

Before you knew it, you were all grown up.
Jaded by life, a soft girl turned tough.

AS CARIBOO EASED against the sides of her legs and purred, she became aware of the unlikeliness of what was supposed to happen. Did she really believe her father was going to read a letter she had written about all the horrible things that had happened and then make a decision to change? For the first time she doubted it very much, and, as she rubbed her sweaty palms against her pant legs, she saw how thought and emotion had carried her away — for the past twenty minutes she had sat on the festering carpet thinking, feeling, hurting — and now she was angry.

She could hear his footsteps and braced herself. She clutched the letter in her hand and as the door swung open her hand reached out, her face flushing. Her father stepped into the room looking disheveled, in the same clothes she had seen him wearing the day before. He smelled of smoke, and in the parlor, it mixed with the smell of the urine in the carpet. She held her breath for fear she might gag. "What's that baby girl?" he asked. Two women followed him from behind and he directed them to the back room.

"It's a letter for you, Dad. Can you read it now?" He eyed her carefully and took the letter from her hand. His foot tapped the floor impatiently as he tore the envelope open and pulled out the carefully scripted piece of paper.

While he was reading, she imagined her father's outstretched arms, his remorse, his clearing out the back room, and vowing that he would change both their lives for good. He would fix things. While he was reading, she imagined a long talk and a home cooked meal and then, as suddenly as he had taken the letter, he was giving it back.

"If it's so bad here, you can find another place to live. We'll talk about this another time," he said, and disappeared into the back room. He shut the bedroom door behind him, and she could hear the sad shrieks of empty laughter telling of situations best left unimagined. Soon from underneath and all around the crooked door crept the familiar smell she knew too well. Something thumped. Her father laughed from down deep in his phlegm choked throat. And music played. Nothing she recognized. It was garbled as though it had been deliberately distorted.

She sat for a long time on the floor where she had written the letter listening to the laughter in the back. The metallic odor that so often filled the air on long nights curled in her nostrils and nauseated her for the last time. Tears streaked her face and soaked the collar of her shirt – but she was not crying for herself.

Finally her desperation turned to strength. She found her peace, rose, and walked out of the front door.

She never once looked back, but through the years would picture Cariboo's tiny face watching from beneath the filthy drapery as she walked away. Alone.

Them

A returned soldier from Iraq, finds himself both enlightened and confused by the American presence there yet even more so by the ignorance of those who have not served—individuals that another veteran of another war chooses to term "citizens." In country, a little girl, her father missing, her brother dead, presses into his hand a necklace. When asked what the charm means, she replies, "Allah." The narrator can never again be the same.

In an American bar, another drinker, a citizen, begins carrying on about "Muslamic radicals," and the narrator responds violently.

He has become one of "Them."

Them

Ryan Smithson

People talk to me about "towel heads" and "terrorists." It's always "us" versus "them." And how are *we* right and how are *they* wrong? People throw this shit in my face because they want it to be validated. Because they think I share their sentiments. Because I'm an Iraq War veteran, and how else would I feel?

Truth is, I did. I hated those people. *Hajis*, that's what we called 'em. *Fuckin' hajis*. We tried to be nice to 'em. We tried to level with 'em, tried to get a good picture of who they are and what they wanted. And they'd betray us. They'd sell us out to the highest bidder in town and then act as double agents. Fuck! Lost good men to tricks like that. So yeah, I hated *haji*. Wanted to kill every last one.

But you spend enough time on the ground in Iraq and you get to know 'em. You still hate 'em, sure, cause you know you can't trust 'em. But you *know* them. You get their culture and their perception. You understand 'em. And you start to learn how ass backwards your own culture is. America. We're the "us." Well, let me tell you, on the other side of the planet, we're the "them."

A guy pops a squat next to me in a bar. I mention that I served in Iraq. Don't usually tell people that. People don't get it. They don't want to understand and I don't want to explain. So I keep it to myself. But, tonight, I've had a few and my tongue's loose. Shoulda seen his eyes light up. Like he just met Neil fuckin' Armstrong. Hey pal, I didn't walk on the moon. I just rode around

35

the desert in a Humvee. But he won't hear it. I'm a hero to this guy, a hero who, he assumes, is as much of a bigot as himself.

So he starts rantin' and ravin' about "these fuckin' insurgents" and "who do they think they are" and "if they got a problem with his country, they should meet him, one-on-one at Ground Zero and fight like men." Can you believe it? *His* country. He actually said that. Like he ever fought for her. And all this time while he's carryin' on about Muslamic radicalists (his words), I'm thinking about this little girl.

SHE CAN'T BE more than nine years old, crouched under a window in her mud-and-bricks home afraid because insurgents have come to her village and are terrorizing the people again. Last week, she watched her older brother bleed to death, stabbed because he wouldn't join their ranks. Her father's been missing since he swore vengeance for his son. We found his body this morning, desecrated and burnt in an alleyway, but I don't tell this little girl that. Now it's just her and her mother, barely getting by. Well, the US cavalry has rolled into town, ladies. My job is to stay with these two broads as my squad kicks down doors looking for the bad guys who won't stop blowing shit up.

And while we sit underneath the window, her mother praying quietly in the corner, this little girl reaches into her pocket and pulls out a gold necklace. It has a charm, an Arabic character, but I can't tell what it says. She looks up at me with these large, brown eyes, takes my hand in hers and places the necklace in it.

"What's it say?" I ask.

"Allah," she says, smiling.

I glance around their tiny house. A few dishes lie here and there. Some old prayer rugs. There's a wooden table and chairs which she tells me her father made. There's some old pots and a stove which barely works. What little food they have sits in a hotel-size refrigerator, and a shelf holds a few books, the only one that's clean at all being a copy of the Koran. This necklace is the only thing with any value, and it sits in *my* hand. Now I know it's an insult to refuse a gift in this culture. But I say, "no" anyway. She smiles, this nine-year-old, and shakes her head. She puts it around my neck and clasps it.

"Yours," she says. "Yours."

I say the only thing I can say, "Shukran"—thank you—one of the few words I actually know in Arabic.

Well we bagged those sons o' bitches that were terrorizing that village, and we sent the survivors down to Abu Ghraib. And that little girl and her mother are alive today because of the god-forsaken US cavalry.

AND THEN, NINE months after I come home, that little girl's charm still hangin' around my neck, I get this drunken cowboy in a bar in Brooklyn who opens his mouth and lets fall out all the filth that composes him. He's yellin' about "hajis" like he actually knows what that word means. He's screamin' about "the liberals who are as much an enemy to freedom as terrorists." He's ramblin' about *them*: Al-qaeda and the Tally-Ban. He's got the whole crowd going and he's goin' on and on about "preserving freedom" and all that other bullshit George W. rhetoric that got us into this mess in the first place.

And all I can think of is that little girl crouchin' under a window, scared to death for her daddy, knowing more about freedom at nine years old than this drunken asshole ever will.

So when my hand leaves its position on my glass of Johnnie Walker and clenches into a fist, I don't regret it. When that fist slices through the air like a missile toward this cowboy's face, I don't regret it. When my knuckles make contact, and I hear that satisfying crunch of his jaw breaking, I don't regret it.

And now here I sit in county jail, doin' my nine-month stint for assault. Here I sit, just one more statistic, just one more soldier whose alcohol-induced aggression becomes just one more reason for the local news media, the public, *us*, to believe that this war just ain't worth its weight in shit.

Well, here I sit, just one more version... of *them*.

Ryan Smithson writes of a young soldier in Iraq whose true passion is tap dancing, whose most cherished memento of who he once was are his "tap shoes." His father, for whose approval and acceptance, he continuously strives is a casualty of 9/11. On a dry highway in Iraq, his Humvee upended by an IED, his fellow soldier, Pvt. Grange mortally wounded, the narrator, in a cloud of rage and dust searches for his rucksack within which lie his precious taps. And then he sees the wires of another device "trailing into the bushes…."

This is not simply a story of war and its dangers. The emotional complexities extend into the past and the future. The world of this soldier's memory and imagination intersect with another reality which some may identify, others not. The tap shoes, however, are as real as "the sting of hot metal."

Tap Shoes

Ryan Smithson

I carry my tap shoes in my rucksack.

They're comfortable there, in their little black bag with the gold pull string. They sit nicely among the green socks and brown t-shirts. Rucksacks are bottomless—you might not know that—so there's always room for my tap shoes. There's a little spot for them right behind my bag of toiletries, my picture of dad. They look good there, in their little black bag. They've traveled the world with me.

At first they stayed in the States, my tap shoes.

MY FIRST PAIR was small. I was five years old, and they felt unnatural.

I practiced, and they got better. I learned ballet, too. A little bit of jazz. Some ballroom. I did recitals, competitions. Mom and dad were proud. Well, mom was proud. Dad was a cop, real man's man. I guess my leotard embarrassed him.

I stuck with tap the longest. Tapped all the way through middle school. Out of all the styles, it was the most fun, the way you almost hover above the floor. It's not so much about "inspiration" or "interpretation" like the other styles. It's raw. It's you and the floor and the beat between them. I loved it, that feeling. All those people watching me from their seats, watching me hover around the stage. I was alive. Really alive.

I could have been a professional, said my teacher. She wasn't lying either.

ONCE I ENTERED high school, the stigma of a boy tapping around in cute little circles, shuffling and prancing about in flashy outfits, became too much.

I mean, I was thirteen. *Time to grow up*, I thought.

So I tried out for football. My footwork was incredible.

"You're a natural running back," said my coach. "Where'd you learn to be so fluid on your feet?"

"Dance class," I said, and the other guys laughed.

I made varsity my freshman year. Went out for basketball, too. Then track in the spring. I excelled in all of them. Guys would find out about my dancing, then laugh. And then they'd watch my magic out on the field, or the court, or the track. Some of them got into dance. They learned ballet. They learned how to tap. They learned jazz. And the jitterbug. All just to keep up with me.

Myself? I was too busy for dancing anymore.

MY DAD DIED in '01, shortly after graduation.

The last time I talked to him, he called me from his hotel in Boston where he was staying for some sort of conference. He'd be leaving for Los Angeles soon, he said, and then off to Dallas for some training that would help him earn his captain bars. I wouldn't see him for a couple months. Welcome to my childhood.

He was always working, always traveling; always missing football games, dance recitals, Christmas...

I said, "Speaking of Boston, Dad, I've been thinking of going to Boston College for fine arts."

He laughed easily and said he wasn't sure about me. He laughed like he was joking. But a young man gets to a point in life when he can tell whether or not his father is joking.

I never saw Dad again, never got to say goodbye.

I didn't go to college. I joined the army. Don't really know why. Dad always talked about his time in the service. It sounded fun and hard and exciting. He never saw combat, but he traveled the world before he met my mom.

I joined the military police. Don't really know why. Thought I might like the police as a career afterward.

Then the war started.

MY TAP SHOES go everywhere I do in Iraq, comfortable there in my rucksack.

They've been to Samarra and Fallujah. They've been to Mosul and Tikrit. They hate the cities, love the villages. They lay anxiously in my rucksack during firefights. And rest quietly on perimeter guard.

Once in a while, they come out of my rucksack, my tap shoes. I try them on. Late in the stillness of night when no one will see, the worn leather hugging my feet like a blanket.

Once in a while, I swing them off the edge of my cot, let them hover above the plywood floor of our tent. Touch down softly: *Tip-tap, tip-tap.* And I look around to see if no one noticed.

Once in a while, I make real contact. *Toe, shuffle, heel, toe-stamp, heel, stomp. Tip, clack-clack, thud, tip-tap, thud, knock.* Until someone stirs in their sleeping bag.

Then I stop.

WE HIT AN IED.

That's how it happens. Out of nowhere. Always unexpected. Picture a hijacked jetliner. Picture men in business suits on their way to meetings, women in floral dresses on their way to leisure. Then bam—out of nowhere—a man with a trigger.

We flip. My rucksack goes flying from the Humvee. I climb from the wreckage. Dust everywhere. And blood. And Private Grange.

I try to keep my head straight. All that training crammed in there. Convoy live-fire exercises. Some infantry sergeant back in the States and his speech about PTSD. Some training NCO who warned us that they'll plant an obvious bomb, then plant another where they think we'll regroup. Don't remain complacent, they said. And all the rest of it.

Well, let me tell you, it all goes out the window when you see one of your soldiers, your gunner, your brother, blown apart. I grab my weapon, yank it from the Humvee, and scream at the top of my lungs.

"You fucking coward!" I yell.

I'm yelling at Haji, the asshole who flipped the switch. I'm yelling at my dad. I'm yelling at...myself.

I charge to the road, stand in the center—the summit of a mountain. I stand like I own the place. Fire burns behind my skull. The Humvee that was riding behind us pulls up. I can hear their engine and their radio crackling orders to some QRF team somewhere.

"You alright?" asks Staff Sergeant Miller.

I stare into the vast desert, turning to see...anything.

"Sarge," says Miller. "You hurt?"

"No," I hear myself say. I am numb, disassociated. "Grange is... Grange is fucked up."

I hear Miller run to our toppled Humvee. I hear myself howl "you fucking coward!" into the air again. I hear gunshots from my own rifle. The sky swallows the bullets. There's nothing around for miles. All I see is the curve of the earth. This ugly, brown thing.

Miller yells for a tourniquet. Someone comes running, a CLS with all that kind of medical shit in a bag around his waist. It's no use. Grange is a goner. I can hear him choking on his own, hot blood. I sprint to the edge of the road and dive, head first, into the bushes.

If you didn't know better, you'd think I was being heroic.

I scramble around on my hands and knees, patting the ground

for any signs of my rucksack.

Someone yells my name. *One minute*, I say to myself. *I have to find them.*

Dust is everywhere. And jungle-like foliage in my face. The dense thud of the blood pumping through my head. Someone yells my name again. It's my dad's voice.

Forget it. Find the rucksack.

I spot a strap. There in the dried up irrigation ditch, like it's been there for centuries, my ruck sits comfortably. I crawl over and set it free. I pat the dust off. It coats the olive green pack like dust coats everything in Iraq.

Hell isn't full of fire and brimstone. It's full of dust.

I rip the top of the ruck open like a Christmas present, and inside there are socks and underwear. There's brown t-shirts and deodorant. There's a Cliff Notes copy of *Hamlet* and a laminated picture of Dad.

From somewhere in the bushes—peculiar—the sound of an airplane. Within my rucksack, the black bag with a gold pull string. I yank it open and feel the sting of hot metal. The bottom of the tap shoes—the thing that gives them life—feels, under this Iraqi sun, like jet fuel igniting.

For the first time, I empathize with Dad. For the very first time, I feel the fear he felt. The intimate fear of watching Manhattan pass so closely beneath his window seat in business class. The brutal fear of seeing a streak of dark smoke in the skyline, a sign of things to come. The dark smoke rolling like eternity.

Somewhere in the bushes, Dad yells my name. I grab tightly the hot metal of my tap shoes, that comforting sting of home, of childhood.

The dusty air settles a bit. And I see the wires now. Off to the right, trailing into the bushes.

From an airplane window, from Eternity, finally, Dad says,

Ryan Smithson

"I'm proud of you."
    Just before the second explosion.

A bounty hunter, enforcer and mercenary, Ronin, has seen every kind of job and every kind of complication. His latest assignment - retrieving a rich family's runaway daughter seemed to be nothing but more of the same. Things quickly take a turn for the worse, however, as Ronin discovers that the girl has managed to involve herself with a legendary figure in the underworld that might just be too big to cross.

Sweet Dreamz

William Schultz

3 A.M.

I would sleep if I could, but I hardly do that anymore. I could eat something too, but I'm not in the mood for anything specific. The rain is like pellets of ice as it hits my face, and my duster might as well be a wet towel wrapped around me. The neon glow of the lights in the club windows nearby is the only light in the alley other than my cigarette. The punk bands are especially bad tonight and it's taking more than my usual level of patience to pretend I can't hear them. I can smell the junkies and pushers cooking Dreamz in the apartments above the clubs and I try to shake it away.

I lean against the slick wall behind me and refocus my attention on the door of the Holy Diver. The 'Dive' as it's called by the locals is about the toughest place in New York to get into these days. A bunch of music executives own the place on paper, but it's all a front for pushing Dreamz. What the Mafia doesn't control of the stuff is limited to small timers in small neighborhoods that are too stupid, too burned or too desperate to know they are messing with someone else's biz. The 'Dive' is where the big players hang out. They decide the distribution, the prices and they settle any disputes. Usually that means they take someone into the basement and cut them into little pieces with a laser-scalpel. The heat cauterizes the wound so you get to suffer for a while, you see.

You'd think no one would come near the place knowing all

47

that, but you'd be wrong. Drugs, money, orgies and the best bands in the city draw plenty of rich assholes with nothing better to do with their money. It also draws idiot kids who think the life is glamorous. The girls end up strippers if they are lucky and sex toys if they aren't. The boys end up as runners or pushers who get sent to the worst parts of town to deal. The ones who don't get whacked get sent to Dr. Bob over in Chinatown for some Chrome and end up as muscle. Chrome is what the street calls cybernetic enhancements these days. They can turn a fifteen-year-old kid into a hyper-fast, hyper-strong killing machine for the cost of a few thousand dollars and about fifty years off your life.

Whatever happens to these kids, they all end up on Dreamz and they all end up dead or wishing they were.

I crush my cigarette out on the wall. I hate this place, but I do what I'm hired to do. I reach into the pocket of my duster and pull out the hologram. The little disc hums and a five-inch tall 3-D image pops up for me to see. Cute kid. She might be twenty, might not. Stephanie Neal, the daughter of a rich aerospace engineer from Long Island. Daddy sent his little girl to Trenton to go to boarding school, but she never made it there. The family paid every P.I. in New York to track her down, but mostly they took the money and stayed the hell away from places like this. Lucky for Mr. Neal, I'm not afraid of much.

Check that. I'm not afraid of a goddamn thing.

Mr. Neal doesn't know me, of course. He and I will never meet. He deals with Stacy, my handler. She has an office and a staff full of desk jockeys in suits with bad haircuts and a secretary and all that. It all looks legit and that makes people like the Neal family feel better even though they know the truth. At least, they think they know.

I wait for a motorcycle to pass by before I cross the alley to the Dive. The pavement is wet and sloppy and littered with porno flyers, beer cans and used needles. A couple of shaved head troglodytes are standing at the door of the Dive watching me as I come at them. They have these smug looks on their faces that I feel like smacking off, but that isn't going to help me. They get a little more serious as I get close and give each other some worried looks. I'm not a small guy. Hell, I'm a monster. At six-foot six and two hundred seventy-five pounds, I tend to scare people - at least people who value their health. The bouncers edge closer to each other, blocking the door.

They are Twitchers; I can see that right away. One of the most popular mods the Mafia gets their enforcers is a reflex trigger. A computer takes over reactions for your nervous system. It makes you faster than any normal human could ever be. It also makes you twitch as your nervous system keeps trying to do its job even though it's been outsourced. They look like they've taken their muscle enhancement cocktails today too and of course they are high, so they'd be more than willing to fight if it comes down to it.

"No more tonight," one of them growls, flashing me a gap-toothed grin.

I pull a hundred out of my pocket and hold it up. "You sure you can't squeeze in one more?"

The bouncer flicks his hand out faster than a blink to take it. I catch his wrist and his eyes all but pop out of his head in surprise. "Open the door and you get the money."

They don't argue.

The Dive is loud. The music is blaring and it sucks and the crowd is even louder. Strippers are dancing in cages all over the dance floor and giving lap dances and other favors in the booths along the walls. A bunch of bars are spread out through the place and the booze, pills and smokes are being passed around easily. A couple of bouncers are beating some kid half to death in the corner for some reason I don't know and don't care about. A couple of nude girls try rubbing up against me, but I push past them. I prefer the type of girl that won't leave me with crotch rot in the morning. People thrust handfuls of drugs in my face as I push my way to the huge, crescent shaped bar in the middle of the room, but I ignore them too. I don't do drugs. Nicotine and alcohol are bad enough.

The bartender waddles over to me. He's an old fat guy with a bushy beard and a pair of mirrored data shades. Data shades are like a heads-up display built into glasses. He can keep track of all of his orders right in front of him.

"What can get you?"

I slap a hundred on the counter. "I'm looking for girl that might be new here." I toss the hologram on the counter and switch it on. "You know her?"

He pauses. He could have gotten away with lying is he hadn't hesitated, but I can smell bullshit a mile away. "Never seen her before. What are you drinking?"

A slap another hundred on the bar. "I'm not a cop," I assure him. "Tell me about the girl."

He leans toward me so that I can see myself in the glasses. "Your money won't help me if I'm dead. Maybe you should go ask Mr. Reed over in the corner if he has a girl that suits you."

He takes my money and hobbles back to the other side of the bar and I turn my attention to the spot he subtly pointed to when he picked up the bills. There's a skinny guy in a five thousand dollar suit surrounded by bodyguards sitting in a booth there. A half dozen girls are hanging all over him and his crew. They're all glassy eyes and giggling, screwed up on Dreamz. None of them looks like Stephanie Neal.

Two of the bodyguards stand up as I get close and I stop, keeping my distance. "Mr. Reed. You and I might be able to do some business."

The guy narrows his eyes at me. "And you are?"

"Ronin."

The two bodyguards all but wet their pants. I have a bad rep on the street. I deserve every word of it too. I don't put up with fools, I always finish my jobs and I tend to kill people who piss me off. Mr. Reed turns whiter than a ghost and starts getting all jumpy.

"Relax. I'm not here to hurt you. I'm looking for this girl."

He looks at the hologram and shakes his head. "She's not one of mine."

"But you know her."

He nods. "She one of Morpheus's girls. Sorry."

Yeah, so am I. I've been in this town my whole life and I've seen it all, but I've never seen Morpheus. He's a legend on the street, the hero of the masses who made the junk that helps them all escape their pointless lives. He's their goddamn god. The god of Dreamz. If he has Stephanie Neal, I'm going to be working for my money.

"I'll need to see Morpheus," I tell him. I'm not much of a negotiator, you see. If I want something, I generally ask for it.

"I can't arrange that," he shoots back.

I ask once. If I don't get what I want, I tend to take it. "Mr. Reed, I came here as a gentleman and I would like to leave as one. If you push me, I have no problem turning this place into a warzone. Now get up, tell your assclowns to sit down and take me to Morpheus."

"He'll kill me."

I am losing my patience now. "Look, if you take me to him, you walk out with me. Maybe he finds you later and kills you. Maybe you get away. If you don't take me to Morpheus right now, I'll tear your damn head off and roll it across the dance floor."

He gets up. They always do. He's shaking like a leaf as we walk to the stairs at the back of the club and start up to the private rooms. The high priced hookers entertain in the rooms. I step over the low priced ones. Mr. Reed is sweating like a pig and glancing over his shoulder at me. Three of his bodyguards are following us, though they think I don't know it. I could really care less. I meant what I said - if he takes me to Morpheus, he can walk away.

Reed takes me to another set of stairs and we keep climbing. I figure we must be at the top floor by now. He knocks on a door at the top and an intercom barks back at us telling us to go away.

"I need to see Morpheus,' Reed stammers. "It's important."

I look up at the camera over the door and wave. To my right, an auto-cannon swivels around to draw a bead on me. It's at least a fifty caliber, maybe bigger. One shot from that beast and I'm going to be in two pieces. I look behind me at the stairs and judge the distance. I figure if I jump as far as I can, I can make it down to the next landing and save my skin. It'll hurt, but it beats dying.

I'm about to do it when I hear the bolts disengage and the door opens. Reed looks as surprised as I am. He flashes me a nervous smile and then starts through the door. I grab his arm and shove him back toward the stairs. I don't need him anymore and I don't need to be distracted. I smell something wrong here. This was too easy. Reed takes the hint and runs back down the stairs.

I step through the door into a room that takes up the whole floor of the building. It looks like some sultan's harem with silk hanging from the walls and a bunch of garish pillows piled everywhere. There's a pool in the middle of the room with a bunch of girls around it all dressed like Persian dancing girls. A few steroid monsters wearing turbans are fanning them with huge palms. In the center of it all is a kid about seventeen lounging on some pillows with a drink in one hand and a syringe in the other. Curled up next to him burned out of her mind is Stephanie Neal. She has a juice port - a permanent injection site - in her arm and the kid is loading her up with Dreamz.

The kid laughs at me like a maniac as I get closer. "You're him?" he asks in a drug-induced haze. "You're the infamous Ronin?"

I look around at the bodyguards. The palms are gone and the four of them have assault rifles complete with silencers and laser sights. The little red dots dance around on my t-shirt. "You can't be Morpheus. You're just a kid."

He laughs again, high pitched and hysterical. "Oh yeah, big man? Just a kid? I got all the juice, brother. I'll be seventeen forever. Before Dreamz, there was Blitz. Before Blitz, there was Legacy. I'm not just the god of Dreamz, my man. I am the Legacy."

It made sense. I can remember stories about Morpheus from when I was a kid. If it is the same guy, he would have to be using something to keep himself young. "I'm not here to screw with you Morpheus. I'm here to take Stephanie Neal home to her parents."

The girl is so spaced out she doesn't even react. Morpheus sits up a bit and shakes his head. He puts an arm around Stephanie and rubs his face on her hair. "Oh no, not my angel." He's whispering the words like a prayer. "My angel stays with me."

I look around again. "Then why I am here? You let me in. I assume you knew why I came. What's your game?"

"Been looking for you," Morpheus says. He fingers a necklace he's wearing. I can't make out what it is exactly, but I notice Stephanie is wearing one too. "Been lookin for the one and only, the worst of the worst, the 'man'. I knew you were coming. I knew what that rocket geek father of hers was up to. I had to fix it. I had to keep my angel. So your job's over. It's done. Don't matter now."

Like I said, I'm not afraid of anything, but this freak is getting me a little edgy. What the hell is he talking about? What did he fix? How could my job be through? I look closer at him and I finally see what's hanging around his neck. My whole body tenses. The necklace is threaded through human eyeballs. The Neals are dead. That's how he fixed it. I can't take Stephanie home, because she doesn't have one anymore.

"You work for me now," he continues. "I bought up that contract. Ms. Stacy at the office said she didn't mind. Ain't that right, Angel?"

Stephanie laughs lightly, her eyes glazed over and staring as she fingers her own necklace. "Right, lover. That's right. Just you and me now, lover."

Stacy. Now that does it right there. I've been a gentleman here. I've tried to play by the rules. Morpheus is still talking and that idiot girl is still laughing. I'm burning. All I can see is Stacy and the picture of the Neal family she showed me. Just some working class people lucky enough to have some money and a nice house and a dream that their kids could have the same. They weren't me. They never hurt anybody. They didn't live this life. They just got on the wrong person's list.

Morpheus is still talking. Stephanie is laughing and kissing his fingers. The four bodyguards are smirking at me, the laser sights trained on my chest. They had it all planned out. They pulled off the perfect job. They got rid of the Neals, they won Stephanie's freedom and they took out my handler. Now they had me dead to rights and at their mercy. The perfect move. Checkmate.

Almost.

I don't have any cyber-shit in me. Not a bit. Cybernetics suck. They set off metal detectors, they show up in x-rays and security scans. Being a former employee of various black ops outfits, I got the liquid version. My internal organs have been modified on a genetic level to secrete the chemicals that make me what I am. And I'm fastest, strongest, meanest and most ruthless son-of-a-bitch on two legs.

A pair of Manhunter pistols are in my hands before the rifle-toting morons even realize it. I empty both twelve shot clips in less than a second and the four of them drop in clouds of crimson mist. The roar of the guns is still echoing through the room as I drop them and pull my Scorpion .44. Morpheus is no slouch he is on his feet with Stephanie in front of him. He has a blade in his hand and is holding it to her throat. She just keeps laughing and telling him she loves him as he starts to back away. The rest of the harem girls scatter.

Before I can do anything, I hear footsteps on the stairs behind me. Reed and his men. I dive behind a table as they open up with sub-machine gunfire. There are four of them counting Reed, all firing like idiots through the room, taking 'spray and pray' over aiming. I pull an apple-sized grenade from my belt and toss it their way. Flesh and steel wither under the force of the blast and I hear screams from the doorway. I'm over another table and rushing through the smoke before they can recover. Reed is dead and so is one of his men. The other two have armored dermal plates and are bloodied but moving. I empty the Scorpion into the first guy and he drops. The second guy swings around with a pistol, but I have his wrist in my hand before he can fire. I bring is elbow across my knee and snap his arm. He screams as bones poke through the skin and grabs at my face with his free hand. I slap the hand away and tear his throat out with my fingers. Blood explodes everywhere and I toss him to the floor.

My ears stop ringing for a second and I can hear Stephanie moaning from back near the pool. I find her kneeling over Morpheus as he chokes on his own blood. His idiot pals peppered him with bullets and he's got a few minutes of agony now before it's lights out. Stephanie bleeding from a gut wound and a shoulder wound, but she's so high she doesn't even know it. I grab her and pull her away from Morpheus to check on her. She screams and fights me, but I ignore her mouth and her feeble kicks.

The shoulder wound is no big deal, but the stomach wound is fatal. Her insides are bulging out and there is nothing I can do about it. There is no place to take her around here and no time to go somewhere else. She's a goner. I pull the necklace with Stacy's eyes on it off her neck and then shove her to the floor.

To hell with her.

I'm picking up my pistols when I see her crawl back over to Morpheus. The bastard is still alive somehow, but it won't be long. She reaches into the waistband of his pants and pulls out a handful of syringes.

"I'll make us better, lover," she tells him in her sleepy, dreamlike voice. "I'll make us all better."

She shoots him up with three syringes and then gives herself a pair. A few seconds later, she laughing again, kissing his face and telling him it will all be okay. She stretches out on top of him and their blood mingles together. Her laughter grows louder and louder as I start back for the stairs. As I start down, I can hear his dying words as they lay in their black embrace.

"Sleep now, angel. Let's sleep. Sweet Dreamz, angel. Sweet, sweet Dreamz."

Edward K. Ryan

Fleeing their former employer, mercenaries Tyris and Stulthius Menion find shelter in a tiny town that seems doomed to fall under the swords of the battling factions in the area. When their warning to the pair of strange children that seem to be the only inhabitants falls on deaf ears, the brothers learn that there are forces in the world stronger than flesh, blood and steel.

The Reckoning

Edward K Ryan

Tyris and Stilthius Menion trudged into Krendor.

Soaked, muddy from head to toe and spattered with dried blood, they looked like men who had dragged themselves directly from a battlefield. The simple farmers and townsfolk of the village would have taken them for the walking dead had there been any such villagers to see them. Their dark faces lined with fatigue and their eyes red with lack of sleep, the brothers stared through the wisps of fog that still hung in the air, straining to see any sign of life in the gloom. Forcing one foot ahead of the other without thought or purpose, the huge men spared no energy to wonder where the people of Krendor were. It did not matter. Not now. They were not making their way to Krendor so much as they were getting away from what lay behind them.

Things had been bad for the brothers for months now. Fleeing their homeland of Tuliny for the island of Kronos had been necessity more than choice. Their entire clan lay dead at the hands of rivals and Tyris and Stilthius were the last of their line. They took their revenge as best they had been able, killing the men who had done the actual murdering and a few others they knew to be behind the planning. Fighting a whole clan alone was a losing fight, though, and the brothers were no fools. Dying in a futile struggle accomplished nothing.

Staying on Tuliny was pointless after that. There were too many men who would be looking for them and too few places to hide for men of their renown. The Menion name was well known and Tyris and Stilthius had made their own names as well. Kronos was a place to start over; a place engulfed by conflict of all kinds where warriors like them would find work. Easy money, Stilthius had once said.

Tyris would have punched his brother in the face for that if he had anything close to the strength for it.

The Three Swords was the name of the last mercenary outfit they had sold their services to. It was a small band of men, a score or so not counting the Menion brothers, but they were a hard bunch. Starting with their captain, one Sular the Red, every one was a true warrior, a professional. They were men who earned their living with swords and traded in blood.

They were also a collection of evil bastards.

That usually suited the brother's just fine. Mercenary work rarely attracted timid men or ignorant idealists who thought they were going to be part of some benevolent crusade to aid the poor and weak. It was about killing people that a wealthy man paid you to kill. Right and wrong didn't mean shit. It was usually about one rich man arguing with another over who owned a herd of cattle or a piece of land or the right to tax a village. The people arguing sent what men they had, hired more when they didn't have enough, and let them hack the hell out of each other until one side ran out of soldiers, money or patience. It wasn't right or wrong. It was just business.

At least to most, Tyris Menion thought as he and Stilthius stopped to look around the pathetic collection of dingy buildings that called itself a village. Unfortunately for the brothers, the Three Swords had decided to take the business of their employer a bit too far.

"You there!" Stilthius called to a boy pushing a wheelbarrow across the street ahead of them. He was the first sign of life they had seen in the sorry excuse for a town.

He stopped at once, staring back at them like he might a wild animal that was preparing to charge him.

"Is there an inn about?"

The boy did not react for a long moment before finally shaking his head. "No inn, sir. Not here."

"No?" Tyris asked, his feet already aching at the thought of moving on to the next village.

The boy shrugged. "Who would stay there?"

Tyris looked about again. He had a point.

"If you need a place to sleep," he went on, "my family has a farm on the east edge of the village. My father might allow you in the barn. He lets travelers sleep in the loft if they can pay or do a day's work. You might have luck."

Tyris looked around them. "Where the hell is everyone?"

The boy shrugged again. "Drunk or recovering from it. Last eve was the feast of Yanrah."

"Yanrah?" Stilthius asked.

"Goddess of wine, music and love. Plenty of all of that last night." He cocked an eyebrow at the brothers. "You looking for a place to sleep or not?"

Stilthius nodded and jerked his head to the east, beckoning his brother to follow. The boy abandoned his wheelbarrow and dashed ahead of them.

"I hope this family of his has beer," Tyris muttered.

"Food," Stilthius mumbled back.

"Blankets and a bath!"

"Pretty daughters!" Stilthius bellowed.

The brothers laughed like mad men until they reached the weather-beaten fence that penned in a collection of hogs.

There were a dozen or so, all great, fat things that wallowed in the mud and did not react to the strangers as they came to lean on the fence. Beyond them, past the promised barn, a pair of cows and a few horses roamed a pasture that stretched back toward the hazy bulk of the forest. The nearby house was a small, simple thing, little more than sagging timber and thatch. A vegetable garden that looked unlikely to yield much of use lay to one side of the well-worn path that led to the door. A girl that Tyris guess was no more than eight looked up from where she knelt at its center, bolted upright at the sight of them and dashed away to the house, slamming the door behind her.

"Scared her, you ugly shit." Stilthius hammered a huge fist into his brother's shoulder.

Tyris elbowed him back and shook his head. A bit taller and heavier than his older brother, Tyris still looked enough like him that people often mistook them for twins. If he was ugly, Stilthius was no less so.

Muted voices carried from the house, too garbled to make any sense of. After a few moments, they went silent and the front door swung open again.

The boy from the street and the girl from the garden emerged. The former met their gaze tentatively. The latter stared at her feet.

"The barn is yours for a day's work or a coin." The boy cleared his throat. "Whichever you choose."

Stilthius looked past them at the still shadows of the house. "Your father doesn't care to see the men who have come to his property?"

The boy shook his head. "My mother is ill. He tends to her." He shifted impatiently. "Do we have a bargain?"

Stilthius worked a hand under his mail shirt and into the pocket beneath. The children stared at the silver coin he produced without the slightest expression. Stilthius tossed it to the boy who caught it with a nod. He looked it over and then passed it to his sister. She ran her fingers over the smooth edges, put the cold metal against her lips and then tucked it into a pocket in her apron.

Though he thought later he had been mistaken, Tyris could have sworn she smiled for an instant. When he focused on her face to be sure, the flat, expressionless mask was back.

He shook the thought away and returned his attention to the boy. "Will that buy us some food as well?"

The boy waved the little girl back toward the house. "I will bring you something."

"Beer, too!" Stilthius called after them.

The door closed without a response.

The brothers piled what meager gear and supplies they still possessed to one side and set about making themselves comfortable in the loft. Their packs were empty save for a change of clothes and a spare pair of boots for each of them. Their blankets, food, water and cooking utensils were still in their saddle bags on the horses the Three Swords had supplied. Two days of steady rain had provided enough to drink on their journey to Krendor, but they had eaten nothing for almost three full days.

They had just stripped off their mail shirts when the boy came to remedy the ache in their bellies. The boy called to them from below and Stilthius waved him up. He climbed with one hand on the ladder and the other on a tattered old bag. When he reached the top, he said nothing, looking the outlanders over carefully. Stripped to the waist, the brothers were huge bear-like men, all muscle and sinew and ugly scars that crisscrossed their earth-brown skin. Tyris guessed the boy might never have seen a soldier in his life and certainly not men like the outlanders.

"Come to brings us food or stare at us like a fool, boy?" Stilthius asked as he pulled off his boots.

The lad gave him a flat, empty look and shuffled over, dropping the sack between them. The brothers tore into it, finding a wooden jug of bitter beer, fresh bread still warm from the oven and a generous portion of dried sausage. Tyris stuffed his mouth full without even looking up at the boy.

"You have a name, son?" Stilthius asked as he uncorked the jug.

"Cale," he answered. The boy looked them over with a critical eye. "Are you Duke Armus's men?"

"Armus?" Stilthius looked to Tyris.

"Duke of Turgin," the younger brother replied through a mouthful of bread. He looked to Cale. "No."

The boy frowned. "We were hoping you were."

Stilthius took a long drink and passed the jug to Tyris. "Why's that?"

Cale shrugged. "Word is men are raiding villages. Lord Densid and Lord Valg have been fighting over territory all year. They say Valg is burning down whatever he can't take and hold. His men burned out Corlich's Ferry a week ago. Easeron a few days past. We're close enough that the folks lucky enough to escape came here. People have been hoping the Duke will send men to put an end to all the fighting."

Tyris lowered the jug and locked eyes with his brother. They knew all about those places. Knew all too well.

"We're just passing through," Stilthius told the boy after a moment. "We don't work for anyone."

"But you said you aren't soldiers," Cale insisted. "That must mean you're sell-swords."

"We don't work for anyone," Stilthius repeated, his voice laced in steel.

The boy nodded and fell silent a moment. His gaze wandered a bit until settling on the two long canvas bundles the brothers had placed with their packs.

"Nothing there you need to concern yourself with, lad," Tyris told him. "Best you run along now. We'll sleep the night and be off. Tell your mother the food is good, we appreciate it."

"My sister."

"Huh?"

Cale pointed to the food. "My sister bakes. My mother's been ill since last winter. My brother Urik, too, but he died. Raiders came like they do now. Lord Densid sent no men then, and people say he's keeping them close to his manor this year, protecting his most important lands. We do not matter to him."

Stilthius snorted and spat. "He's just out of men and money. Those two bastards have been at this so long they fight because they don't know how to stop."

The boy looked them over a moment, hoping, it seemed, that they had more to share or something to offer in the way of comfort, but the brother's ate and drank and said nothing. Finally, Cale sighed, cast a long glance at the canvas bags again, and left them, disappearing down the ladder.

The Menions finished their meal in silence and settled into their bed of straw. Tyris lay awake for a time, staring up through the cracks in the roof where slivers of pale light seeped through. The moon, his people believed, was the great ivory shield of Hunnaris, the war god. He was also a god of courage, struggle and death. Tyris wondered why his light fell on this place at this hour.

"They'll come here," he said finally, still staring up at the roof.

Stilthius grunted and shifted a bit. "Here and a dozen other places. Valg won't stop until he's punished Densid – hurt him as much as he can. He'll burn everything and then watch the people of this land starve in the fall when there is no harvest. You know the way."

Tyris closed his eyes against the moon light. "Yeah. I know."

They gathered their gear at first light and climbed down from their beds in the loft. They could have used the loft for two nights, but the Menion brothers knew what was coming and how soon. Another day here would be a day too long.

The little girl was back in the garden, trimming and weeding, her apron already filthy and her hands caked in dirt. Tyris spotted Cale in the field behind the barn gathering up the horses. He wished for a fleeting moment that he and his brother could buy a pair, but they had very little money between them and all of it would not have been enough for one animal let alone two.

The girl looked up a moment, her eyes empty and dull. Stilthius raised a hand in greeting, but she looked away without responding. He glanced around once more, flashed his brother a grim look and turned away.

Tyris started after him and then stopped, looking back to where Cale stood just beyond the barn, lead ropes in hand, watching the strangers. Stilthius took a few more steps before realizing he was not being followed and glanced back.

"Coming or not?"

Tyris looked from the little family to Stilthius and back a half dozen times, words forming and evaporating over and over. His brother drifted back and leaned close. "What is it?"

Tyris shook his head. "They know."

Stilthius jerked him around so that the farmers could not see their faces. "What the hell are you talking about?"

The bigger man nodded back to the family. "The boy knows Valg's men – the Three Swords among them – are burning villages. But here they are weeding the damn garden. Why? The Three Swords are twenty-two men. That would be too many for this village even if there were anyone around. But there isn't. And where the hell is everyone? These two are the only people we've seen. No one made a sound all night. No dogs barking. No drunk fools screaming at each other or fighting. Nothing."

The brothers turned to look around at the other farms that dotted the edge of the town. Barely visible in the shadows of the morning half-light, they were dark, silent lumps. No wagon rolled along the earthen paths in the town behind them. No shod hoof beat the ground. No bells or horns or anything to call a gathering of men or signal an opening market.

The little girl stood and faced them. Her pale face was calm and her eyes steady as she fixed them with an even stare. There was an intelligence there that went far beyond a little girl's. To their left, Cale had arrived, the horses milling behind him, forgotten. He too watched the brothers with a cold stare.

"Valg's men are chasing you," Cale told them, his voice steely, sharp and all wrong for a boy or ten or twelve.

Tyris's hand slipped down to the dagger that hung from his belt. "Who are you? How do you now that?"

"We are the last of the people of Krendor," the little girl announced as she went to stand with her brother. "Valg's men destroyed our village, killed everyone and everything. Only the buildings remained. Cale and I came back here to wait."

"Lyss!" Cale snapped, his face pinched with anger.

She shook her head at them "They are not Valg's men. They spoke the truth. Even if my magic fails me, and it does not, they have done us no harm."

"Magic?" Tyris took a step back. Beside him, Stilthius had one hand in the canvas bag he carried, reaching for a weapon.

The girl's hand came up slowly. "Be still, outlanders. You have come in peace; we intend that you should leave in peace. We mistook you for raiders when we saw you on the road yesterday. We intended to give you shelter and murder you in your sleep." She spoke of it as though it were a trivial thing. "My magic looked into your hearts and saw the truth of you, though."

The truth, Tyris thought as he stared at the strange children, was closer to their first impression than they cared to believe.

"Is it?" the girl called Lyss asked, cocking her head at him.

Tyris started and glanced at his brother. He had not spoken the thought aloud. How could she-?

"Know what you think?" she finished for him. "Magic, I said."

"My sister," Cale explained, "is the daughter of powerful spirits. Spirits of vengeance."

Stilthius looked around them. "You are children. Farmers. There is no magic at work here."

Lyss gestured to the horses Cale had left near the barn. "Five of Valg's men rode in on those two weeks ago." She pointed to the hogs in their pen. "Before that, a man claiming to be a merchant tried to rob us and have his way with me. What was his is now ours. Men roam these roads with hearts for theft, rape and murder. Beasts prey on animals and humans throughout these forests. Think you that two simple children remain here by their own wits?"

"We-," Stilthius began.

"Belonged to Valg once," she went on. "You took his coin and spilled blood in his name. You no longer do. That, I think is why his men chase you. That is why you still live. The blood on your hands may yet doom you, outlanders, but not here. Not now. Take your lives and go. You are not our enemies."

Tyris shook his head, still trying to make sense of what he was seeing and hearing. "These men – Valg's men – are cutthroats and butchers. There are a score of them or more. You need to leave this place. They won't care that you are children. They take no pity."

Cale's expression did not change. "We wait for them here. You need to go." He looked from them to his sister and back. "Now."

Tyris began to object again, but Stilthius seized his arm. "Enough. Let us leave this place. If they are what they say or just mad, it is no concern of ours. Better we are as far from here as we can be."

"We could use those horses-," Tyris began.

"They stay." Lyss pointed to the faint dirt path that led north to the other farmsteads and the forest that edged the town.

The brothers hitched up their packs and left without another word.

"Probably just mad little shits," Stilthius declared for the tenth time by Tyris's count.

The brothers had been walking for most of the day, picking their way through the forest a few yards off the edge of the road that snaked through the trees on its way to the city of Kirin Forge. They were several days away still and wary of Valg's men and the Three Swords particularly. Staying off the road was the safest way, but it was costing them time. Tyris was hungry and tired and trying not to think about anything beyond pushing through as best they could.

"They could have just been the last of their family after everyone else with a brain fled the place. The parents could have gotten sick and died or fallen to brigands or beasts," Stilthius mused as they walked. "Magic my ass!"

Tyris only nodded along as his brother rambled and said nothing.

It continued on for the remainder of the day like that, Stilthius talking and Tyris pretending to listen. By nightfall, they had fallen silent and huddled into a spot among the exposed roots of a tree to rest. It was warm enough, the early days of summer now, and the sky was nothing but bright stars and moonlight. They ate a few scraps of food they had saved from what the children had given them in Krendor and rested their heads on their packs.

They had been silent for a long time when Stilthius turned toward him, his dark face a muddled shadow in the filter moonlight. "One thing doesn't make sense."

"One?" Tyris snorted.

"If they had the power to kill us – real or imagined - why let us go? She said we had blood on our hands. Hell, it wasn't us that destroyed her people, but it could have been."

Tyris found himself nodding along with his brother's thoughts. "I think she knew that was why we left Sular and the rest. I think something told her.." He paused. "Maybe that coin she seemed so happy to have," he mumbled, almost to himself.

Stilthius's hand shot out to grip his arm. "You saw that too? I thought I imagined it! It was like she could read something from it like those mad charlatans with their cards and bones." His hand relaxed and lifted away. "Suppose it doesn't mean shit anyway. We're gone and it's done. Best we forget all that nonsense and worry about finding more work when we reach Kirin Forge."

"Keep watch," Tyris told him. "I'll get some sleep and then relieve you."

Stilthius yawned and nodded. There was another long silence. "Tyris?"

"Yeah?"

"We were right. Leaving the Three Swords, I mean. I know we're broke and have no roof over our heads now, but we were right. All that shit Sular and the rest were doing – raping, killing and burning – that was not soldier's work. Not when you're killing farmers and shepherds and... you know."

Tyris turned to look at him. "I know."

"Hunnaris punishes those who prey on the weak. Punishes warriors who do not seek worthy challenges."

Tyris nodded. "One day, Hunnaris will see to a reckoning for those filthy shits for what they've done. He'll see to it."

Stilthius drew a deep breath and let it out slowly. "Yes, he will." He rose. "Sleep well."

Tyris watched his brother pace away, the canvas bag holding his weapons clutched in his hands. Stilthius was many things, not the least of which was a man of faith. What he had seen, what the Three Swords had done, had tested that faith. For his own part, Tyris didn't worry much what some god who had never done much to help or hurt him thought. If it made Stilthius feel like there was a purpose to what went on, he figured that was a good thing .

Of course, nothing he had seen in the last few weeks was made any better by the thought that some god watched over it all.

He looked up through the screen of branches and leaves at the slivers of moonlight. Stilthius had never asked much for his faith. He lived the Tulin way, a warrior way, and asked only that he receive his reward for that in the next life. Tyris was less sure about the whole arrangement. The next life might await or might not. He did his best as he made his way in the world, his brother constantly preaching the right and wrong of what he did. Tyris figured he wasn't likely to get anything in return save for keeping his brother happy.

In the few moments before he fell asleep he offered up a small prayer to the god of the moon that he could not be sure was bothering to listen. For himself he asked nothing. For his brother, he wished Sular the Red and the rest of the Three Swords a long, painful death.

It was past midnight when Stilthius shook him awake. His older brother said nothing, simply pointing south with a grim look. Tyris rose to stand with him, immediately catching sight of what had drawn Stilthius's attention. To the south, the clear sky was burned orange and red with fire and the last bits of the village of Krendor rose to the stars in plumes of smoke.

He spat and turned his eyes to the hazy pale light of the moon.

"Piece of shit."

Stilthius looked over at him. "Eh?"

Tyris waved a dismissive hand in the direction of the burning village and turned away in disgust.

The Menion brothers rode into Krendor three weeks later with fifty men as the full moon rose up over the forests to the east.

The Black River Mercenaries, a huge, powerful group of sell-swords employed by the Duke of Turgin himself had been hired to settle the fighting between Lord Densid and Lord Valg for good. Too many villages had been raised, crops destroyed and people put to the sword. Duke Armus had seen and heard enough. Valg and Densid both had been seized by his soldiers and cast in irons until Armus decided who was responsible for what. Black River was now sweeping the area, rooting out pockets of soldiers and mercenaries who either did not know the fighting was over or had turned to banditry in the face of their employment drying up.

Tyris and Stilthius had been recruited in Kirin Forge soon after arriving. Within the week they had seen their first combat against a dozen of Valg's men who had taken refuge in a nobleman's manor and helped themselves to his food, money and women. Their skill and thirst for fighting had impressed the men of Black River quick enough and the outlanders were already well respected.

It was that respect that enabled them to convince their Captain, a short, scarred man name Shaddix, to look in on Krendor on their way south.

Nothing remained of even the pathetic little hole they had seen weeks before. Every building was a pile of charred rubble. While the men of Black River stopped to rest and collect water from a nearby stream, Tyris and Stilthius picked their way through the shattered town to the farmstead at the eastern edge. The barn with its hogs and horses was completely destroyed. Among the ruins were the corpses of armored men, most still clutching their weapons. They were charred beyond recognition to most, but Tyris and Stilthius knew the armor and weapons of the men of the Three Swords.

More men littered the ground near the burned out shell of the house, twisted and broken atop the ruined little patch of ground that had been Lyss's vegetable garden. The brothers spoke not a single word as they sifted through debris, checking for bodies. Everyone here was a grown man. Every single one.

They worked their way to the back of the house, searching still for any sign of the two strange children they had encountered.

A dozen yards from the house, against a tall, thick willow tree, they found Sular the Red, Captain of the Three Swords. He was upright and facing them, his lifeless eyes staring. He had not been burned like the rest, but his body was bonded with the tree somehow, interwoven in such a way that the trunk ran through him like bones and veins. One arm was consumed by the willow, the other was stretched out before him, reaching, the fingers curled like claws.

Tyris looked the mangled body over and then turned to his brother, but Stilthius only shook his head. There was no explanation for this. No words.

Behind them, they heard Shaddix calling. There was nothing here. Nothing to see or save. They were moving on.

Tyris looked up at the cloudless sky and sighed. The moon would be bright enough tonight. They would make good progress. Stilthius's hand gripped his shoulder and began to pull him away. He cast a last look at the gruesome remains of Sular the Red as he turned and caught a flutter of movement behind the twisted mix of flesh and wood. He beckoned to Stilthius and rounded the big willow to see what it was.

Hanging from one of the branches, flapping gently in the wind, was a dirty little apron. Mixed with the dried mud and grass stains was the familiar tint of old blood.

Stilthius ran his fingers over the soiled fabric. "Hers, do you think?"

Tyris looked all about them, at the shattered town, the charred corpses and the tortured remains of Sular the Red. "No. Not a chance."

His brother did not look convinced. "Killed them all then?

Killed them with her magic?"

The big outlander shrugged. "I know nothing of magic."

He turned his eyes to the full moon. There had been a reckoning for the Three Swords. How and why, were questions he decided to leave for the gods.

With one last look around at the battered remains of Krendor, Tyris Menion left the filthy little apron flying from the tree limb in the wind and followed his brother away.

From the depths of the shadows in the nearby trees, a little girl with cold, empty eyes watched them go.

For an instant, the wind shook the tree limbs above her and let a thin sliver of moonlight touch her face, illuminating what might have been a smile.

The Mercury Project is a multi-generational exploratory mission to reach the Virgo Overdensity on the edge of the galaxy. The all female crew is propagated by a cache of carefully selected frozen embryos; the explorers are sustained by minimal necessities and the glory of being part of the greatest scientific experiment humanity has ever embarked upon.

When Mercury 24 is born a male, it is the first in a series of hurdles the crew must face. Dwindling supplies and a political cover-up hundreds of years behind them may have sabotaged their mission.

Can The Mercury Project be salvaged? Should they abandon the voyage they have been on for twenty-three generations? Can they ever return home?

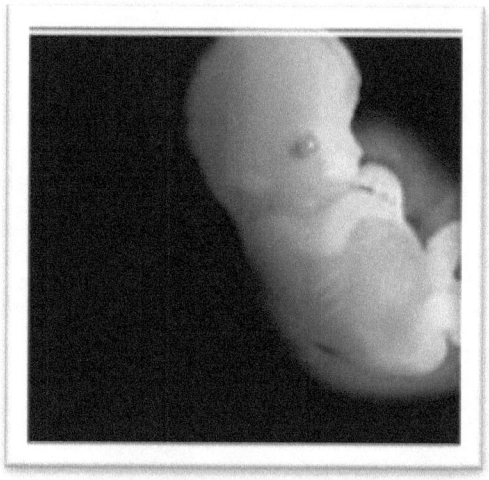

Mercury Shining

Colleen Maloney

"Mercury 23- weight 3.084 kilograms. Height 46.21 centimeters- just a peanut really. Gender female, of course. Both mother and daughter are doing well, no complications during delivery. Termination of Mercury 21 in 3,650 Earth days. Mercury 21 out." Elena swiped the comlink off and cradled her head at the finality of it. Ten years and still so much to do. "Plenty of time to think about that later," she said aloud, mostly for the sake of distraction. "Time to check on the wee one." She made her way through the narrow metal corridor crowded with bulkheads and equipment, insulating her from the cold, unforgiving nothingness outside. Finally, she emerged into the medroom where her daughter sat holding her newborn.

Audrey was brilliant, like all the Mercuries, a brain charged with decoding the universe. But no amount of intellect or clarity of logic could withstand the onslaught of joy she felt for the child in her arms. "I think I'll call her Sadie," Audrey, or Mercury 22 as she was known to science, said.

"The vial said her name was to be Rachel," Elena said flatly.

"Who will know? Her genetic parents are long dead. She's mine now. My little Sadie." She stroked the top of the infant's head. Black hair swirled around her scalp like waves. Her closed eyes were encased in thick, dark lashes. Her skin was a warm, pale brown that would only deepen in richness and tone. She came from a world she would never know, except through data files, her birth coming hundreds of years after her parents had placed her frozen beginnings on board this spaceship, in joyful anticipation that she would be part of the greatest scientific voyage of all time.

"She's not yours. You need to remember that. You need to remember the mission. We can't get caught up in emotion. She is the product of genius and needs to be grounded if this mission is to succeed. One link-"

"Can break a chain, I know mother. Here, just hold your granddaughter." Audrey handed the sleeping bundle to Elena who cradled her like a delicate instrument.

She remembered when Audrey had been born, how she had tried not to become attached to the strawberry-blond girl in her arms. It was difficult at times, and eventually she gave in and let Audrey call her 'Mom.' Still, she had tried to maintain an air of professionalism, albeit a less sterile variety than mandated by Mercury 20.

"Sadie, is it?" Elena said to the infant in her arms. Sadie opened her eyes as if in response to the name. "Well, it seems you agree. Sadie it is." Elena's heart softened a little. "Your father was a famous botanist and your mother, a great mathematician." She sang to her as if doing so would enable the infant to understand. "And you will be a great astrophysicist like the rest of us."

Sadie grunted and bubbled in Elena's arms.

"Ok, maybe engineering will be your specialty. We have a long way to go yet. Another 482 generations at least: to the Virgo overdensity and back again. It is a place where another galaxy is merging with our own. Stellar drama, luckily at an infinitely slow pace. The child squirmed against her swaddled blanket. "No worries little one, there is plenty to keep us busy. There are planets to categorize, anomalies to analyze and more beauty than we have time to measure. You are part of history my dear, a valiant explorer in a long chain of women. Now, let's change that black matter in your nappy, shall we?"

As time passed, despite Elena's best efforts, and Audrey's

meager attempts, it grew difficult to keep Sadie's joy from infecting their hearts. She was a light in the darkness. She found wonder in the universe. She sang while she worked, sculpted water in the zero-g room and painted with her nutrient paste. By the time she was eight, she had decided that science and art were one and the same, that one could not survive without the other. "We don't have to look into the depths of space," she said. "The answers are right in front of us, like echoes of how the universe was put together. The universe is held together in the cosmic web. Spiders have been spinning similar webs for millions of years. It was staring us in the face all along. We just weren't looking." And though her insight might have seemed to be made more of wishes and fairy dust, she was a genius and she was usually right. What was more, she could prove it. With cold hard science or sterile formulas or tea leaves if you liked.

SO WHEN THE day came to say goodbye, it wasn't the mission or the volumes of unfinished research that filled Elena's mind. It was Sadie, or rather the loss of her. She made them all feel alive. Now she hoped Sadie was right, that there was something about life that extended beyond the limitations of a physical body, that somehow Sadie's love would carry her there.

"Grandma, don't think of it as the end, it's just a change. Like rocks or butterflies or drops of rain." Sadie's dark hand wrapped around Elena's pale one. Her warm brown eyes welled up with tears. Saying goodbye was still hard, even if you believed your energy didn't end with death. "I love you, Grandma."

Elena knew why she had to go. The ship only had enough air, food and water to support two adults comfortably. From the moment Sadie was born there was a compromise in resources. If the eldest Mercury survived to the child's tenth birthday, she would take a pill and terminate. On paper, it made sense. But Sadie knew paper didn't make good science.

"I love you too, sweet one. You are so brilliant, the smartest of the Mercury Project. You will do great things."

Her death would allow Sadie to shine. She was a gift to the world, and no one would know about her for years. Elena placed a small pill in her mouth and chased it with a gulp of water. "I hope your theory is right," she smiled.

"We'll meet again," Sadie assured her.

Audrey gripped her mother's free hand and Sadie's reached out to Audrey. They were a circle, but only briefly. Elena shuddered a minute and fell empty. Sadie whispered, "Goodbye, Grandma."

Audrey closed her mother's eyes and tried to stay strong for Sadie's sake. She didn't really buy into this transformation idea her young daughter clung to in the face of death, but it brought Sadie great comfort, so she didn't protest. Audrey lifted her head and took a deep breath, "Come on kiddo, it's best to get this over with."

The girls took Elena's body and placed it in the matter reclaimer. "It seems so strange, tossing your mother in the bin." Audrey was trying not to cry.

"Don't be sad, mother. The best part is gone. It's just matter now."

"Yes, you're right, as usual."

"MERCURY 24-WEIGHT 3.7 KILOGRAMS, height 52.13 centimeters, gender male. Termination seems the only option. Will reimplant Mercury 23 in six weeks. Mercury 22 out."

Audrey punched the control panel. How could this have happened? A male. Equipment on the ship was limited. There was no visual monitoring device to confirm the health or gender of the fetus. They had been assured that the ship had been stocked with female embryos only. Still, it didn't surprise Audrey. Sometimes it seemed like the ship had been supplied by a room full of number crunching budget slaves who didn't waste time or money on double checking things. Mercury 12 had developed cancer due to a faulty gene sequence, leaving her to the ravages of a disease that had been cured for hundreds of years. There was no treatment available, and Mercury 13 was made commanding officer at just 16. But this? How could they have let this slip by? How many more males were on board? It would crush Sadie. Best to get the necessary over with and beg forgiveness after.

Audrey slowly wound her way back to the medroom. "Sadie, how are you feeling?"

"Fine, just fine." She smiled at the little one wrapped in her embrace. "I think I'll call you Moses. Just like Moses, you were cast adrift and left to die."

"Let me see him." Audrey carefully took the baby up in her arms, and quickly pressed a button on the side of the bed. Restraints came up over Sadie's arms and legs, pulling them to the mattress.

"What are you doing?" Sadie struggled against the robotic cords.

Audrey steeled her heart, walked to the counter and picked up a hypo spray.

"Mother, no!" Sadie screamed. She knew what was imminent. It was protocol to terminate a defective Mercury. But this was her son, and it was unacceptable.

Audrey unfolded the blanket Moses was wrapped in.

"Don't please, please!" Sadie begged. Her arms pulled at their bindings. Her eyes pleaded; her wrists burned raw and began to bleed.

Audrey lifted the hypo spray.

"There is another way. Mother please! My baby...my baby." She heaved great sobs.

Moses opened his eyes. Audrey's heart softened in the light of his golden brown gaze and she dropped the deadly instrument.

She wrapped Moses up and held him to her chest. "It is the right thing to do. But I just can't do it." Tears coursing down her cheeks, she looked at Sadie. Audrey retraced her steps to her daughter's bedside and quickly released her, as if immediate action could erase her regret. She handed Sadie the boy. "I'm sorry. I'm so sorry." Sagging to the deck, Audrey wept "Your grandmother was right. I let myself get too attached. I just.... I can't do it."

Sadie gripped Moses tightly. She couldn't tell if her mother was apologizing to her or to the mission or both. The directives they had, pounded into their brains from birth, in the end could not persuade Audrey to destroy something so pure and perfect. Moses was safe, and Sadie knew that anger would do nothing to heal the situation. She looked at her mother, crumpled on the floor. "Love isn't wrong," she soothed. "Our emotions protect us from destruction. Random happenings, like Moses, occur for a reason. The more we learn about the universe the less random we realize it is. The fact is that Moses is here now. We simply have to work him into the calculation."

"That's just it, Sadie." With an air of resignation, Audrey rose and sat on the bed beside her daughter. "With this... complication, we will need to produce another Mercury as soon as possible. We don't have enough resources to support four people. The air circulator and water recombinator weren't meant to handle more than three. Even if you could revamp them to make them more efficient, the nutrient paste won't last the entire mission unless we follow the stated guidelines. It just won't work out."

"Mother, I've been doing some research. I didn't want to worry you, but now it's inevitable. We are a long way out from the overdensity. I'm not even sure we can get there, no matter how many Mercuries are cryopreserved. I checked in storage. There is only enough nutrient paste to last fourteen more generations. The mission is doomed. It's time to revamp more than the air circulator."

"Sadie what are you saying? Abandon the mission? We've come so far. All the other Mercuries will have lived in vain if we abort now."

"Not abort, mother. Change. This experiment has too many variables to make it viable in anything but the planning stage. You know paper doesn't make good science. On this mission we have found twenty-three planets capable of supporting human life. All we could do was send information back to Earth. We couldn't even waste the fuel to land. In the end, you and I both know this ship might as well have been hurtling in space sending data back with no one in it. The original mission is unsustainable."

"Sadie, are you suggesting we colonize a planet?"

"Why not? Why can't we be happy? I want to feel grass beneath my feet. I want to see birds fly and animals and sunsets and smell flowers. Do you know I read that food is supposed to taste good? Imagine looking forward to meals. We have nearly one thousand frozen embryos on this ship. That is plenty for genetic diversity."

"They're all female. *That* is unsustainable." Audrey crossed her arms the way she did when Sadie put too much art in her science.

"All except for Moses," Sadie smiled coyly as she did when she proved that science was art.

"One male? The relations would be too close."

"Maybe Moses wasn't an oversight. Maybe he was put there, intentionally. Maybe there are more."

"That is an awfully big maybe."

"No, it's a puzzle, and we need to find the answer. Don't you think it's strange that this Mercury has a mother whose first name is Marilla and a father whose last name is Cronos?"

"I must admit, Cronos is an odd name. Marilla, what is so strange about that?"

"The root of Marilla is mar — the sea. And Moses' name was supposed to be Aphrodite."

"Who was born when Cronos threw the sky god's testicles into the sea." Audrey's face went pale as the pieces fit themselves together in her mind. She cleared her head. "Perhaps it's just in homage to the parentage, which was merely coincidence."

"I was researching the parental background before Moses was born. I thought, like you, that Aphrodite was just a play on the parents' names. But now that *Aphrodite* is a boy, it all makes sense. Marilla Walsh was one of the head researchers for the Mercury Project," Sadie continued. "Someone knew that we were bound to fail and snuck Moses on board. They left us a way out. I'm sure there are more."

"Sadie, it's been an emotional and trying day. Let's just sleep on it and see how this situation looks in the morning." Audrey's reassuring tone couldn't quell the nagging truths in Sadie's observations. She walked past her sleep chambers and went to the research lab.

IT WAS ONLY days after Moses was born that a persistent clunking in the aft bulkhead woke them up from their sleep.

"It's the water recombinator. If it's not one baby, it's the other."

"I can get it, Sadie," Audrey called out sleepily.

"No, I've got it. I can fix it in my sleep. Keep an eye on the boat rocker for me." She checked on Moses in his basinet and made her way to the bulkhead.

She lifted a panel and squeezed into the narrow slot supposedly meant to accommodate an adult. However, it hadn't been a comfortable fit since she was thirteen. "Ok, old girl, what is it now." This was a problem different from the usual rotted gaskets and parts loosened by solar storms. "Here we go, part of the centrifuge is banging because...." She picked up the metal tether. "You aren't supposed to break, ever." She held the end of the frayed poly coated titanium alloy cord and inspected it. She pulled out her magnifier to take a deeper look. All the cords were frayed but one, which had obviously been clean cut as if with a file. "Well, I'll be. One nick and you'd last about 680 years, I guess. Just enough time for Moses to come to light." She put down the cord. "That means," she looked around the immediate area for some clue and then carefully lifted the cap to the centrifuge compartment. Inside was an engraving. At first it looked like a company logo. She brought her magnifier to the etching. *Gardening: a Beginner's Guide by Marilla Walsh.*

"Genius! You're my kind of woman Marilla."

Sadie quickly fixed the recombinator. It wasn't a difficult fix, but her mind eagerly gnawed at this next clue. It took all of her discipline to keep to the task at hand. As soon as the last nut was in place, she made her way to the cockpit and searched the digital library for the file.

There were no fewer than 276 files by that name, but only one by Marilla Walsh. Sadie couldn't breathe as she opened the document. But eagerness did not spoil her method. Page by page she analyzed it, looking for clues in the table of contents, the way the chapters were organized, repeated words, patterns in spacing, anything.

By the time she reached page 462, she was nursing Moses while Audrey ran morning diagnostics. "Mom," she called out, "look at this."

Audrey placed one arm around Sadie while she looked over her shoulder at the screen. "It's a diagram of the ship. She tucked it in the file. That's not right though," Audrey pointed to a small section on the spacecraft just below one of the storage compartments. "There is an extra compartment there." With a few swipes on the other view screen, Audrey pulled up the official diagram of the ship. "See, that small rectangular compartment isn't on the official diagnostic blueprint."

"Let's see if it's on the official ship." Sadie was grinning as her mind devoured the unfolding mystery. She brought up the outside view of the ship and directed the nearest camera-bot to the location on the diagram. The vision of a tiny box, smaller than the one in the diagram, and obviously welded to the outside of the ship, whet their appetites for discovery.

"Should we get the bots to cut it open and bring it through the air lock?" Audrey asked, getting ready at the controls.

"No, let's go at it from the inside."

"Cut through the hull of the ship? What if the weld isn't secure? It's nearly seven hundred years old."

"If it's not secure I'll just throw a bubble patch over it," Sadie replied nonchalantly, as if a hull breach was no more threatening than a leaky faucet. "Besides, do you think Marilla would have gone through all of this trouble just to make a faulty weld?"

"I can't even imagine the difficulty she had getting all of this in place. It's against everything the project stood for. There was to be no turning back. No diverting from the mission objective." Audrey rubbed the back of her neck, her comfort with Sadie's idea and Marilla's plan was starting to wane.

"She was smart to tuck it in all of the storage compartments." Sadie was ready for the adventure. "Apparently it went unnoticed."

"Sometimes the best place to hide is in plain sight."

Holding the small torch, Sadie crept into the storage compartment. "Here goes everything," she said as she started to burn away at the wall of the ship. As soon as the hull was compromised, she could hear the air suck into the compartment behind. She put down her torch and readied the bubble patch, but the sound was brief. "A vacuum box. Whatever is in there was meant to go into long storage." She took up her tool and began again. It was a long process. The strong smell of bubbling metal surrounded her and penetrated her ventilator. The heat from her labors made her brow drip with sweat. Her knees ached, frozen in their position, but she persevered, so intent on discovery that no amount of discomfort could dissuade her from her task.

Finally, it was done. The metal disk fell to the floor with a resounding clunk. The weld outside had held. She reached her hand into the opening, just large enough to allow its entrance, and pulled out a small envelope. She started to lift the flap but stopped. "Mom will want to see this." She placed the bubble patch on for the sake of precaution, its pale blue gel sealing the wound in the ship. She gathered up her tools and ran the twisted walkways back to the lab.

She could hear Moses' cries echoing down the corridor, crowding everything else out of her mind. She placed the tools and the envelope on the table and gingerly took her son up to nurse. Instantly he was soothed. It amazed Sadie the strength of instinct still intact in humanity. The drive for survival, not just of self but also of family, was a force equal to any that could be unleashed by the universe through which they traveled.

"I haven't opened it yet. I wanted us to do it together," Sadie beamed.

"Suppose it's poison," Audrey suggested, "or some contagion. Perhaps we ought to perform some tests."

"My incredibly unscientific intuition says it isn't dangerous," Sadie replied sarcastically. "Besides, if we run a round of tests the suspense will literally kill me."

"I've been doing some reading while you were gone, on a hunch of my own." Audrey sat at the table, the envelope still unopened before her. "This mission, as you have said, does not appear to be sustainable. News reports from the time of the design suggest that drone ships had been sent ahead of the Mercury Mission. It was said that we would be able to intercept them and resupply."

"What ships? Even if drones had been sent, there are far too many variables in such a long flight. That is one of the reasons the mission had to be manned."

"That isn't all Sadie. The entire first planning team was replaced. The mission was scrapped for apparent budget reasons and then resurrected ten years later, supposedly after the drones had been sent."

Sadie was dumbfounded. "I have read most of the articles about the Mercury Mission and I don't recall any of this."

"I found more. They are the same articles you read as a child, but apparently the information we had was edited. I looked on page 462 of the other gardening books. In three of them I found the uncensored articles."

"How did you ever think to do that?" Sadie asked.

"It's what I would have done," Audrey shrugged. "I also found this." She picked up the tablet and brought it to Sadie.

It was a list of scientists who had first worked on the Mercury Mission. "Wait, the e's in this name are in a different font than the other names," Sadie observed. "Jorge Torres. Is that your papa's real name?" Sadie cooed to the now sleeping infant in her arms. A bead of milk rolled down his cheek, he lay oblivious to the spectacle unfolding around him.

"We know Marilla was part of the second team, so it must have been a joint effort between them." Audrey picked up the envelope and sighed. "The question remains, were they giving us a way out or ending our misery?"

Sadie gently lowered Moses into his basinet. "Remember when I was born? You would have done anything to protect me. I know that because I felt it when Moses was born. We are programed to survive, not just as individuals, but as a species. The love we have for our children is proof. Marilla is protecting her son and his guardians."

Audrey turned over the envelope. "Let's open it." Carefully she lifted the paper flap and peered inside. She pulled out a small paper and laid it on the table. Secured to the paper, in circles of various sizes, were seeds.

"Seeds?" Sadie was astounded. She let out a small laugh. "And I had to read most of a beginner's gardening book to find them."

"It's numbers," Audrey said completely focused on the dots before her. "It's a pattern. Co-ordinates. They are co-ordinates."

They counted the seeds several times to insure they had the numbers right and then entered them into the navigation system.

Sadie's heart was pounding. "It's a planet," she said quietly. "And it's close."

Crushing silence filled the room. This was it. The end of the quest, the final clue decoded. Would they remain faithful to the Mercury Project or begin on this new mission? Would they abandon a doomed scientific voyage that they had been born to carry out or seize this opportunity to propagate their species in a new place despite the possibly of disastrous failure? In the end it was an easy choice.

Audrey put her hand on Sadie's shoulder. "Let's go for it."

Sadie smiled. "I hope some of those seeds are strawberry."

They were three months, six days and 14 hours away from Keplar 22-b, a planet that had been suspected to be hospitable for hundreds of years by the time the Mercury Mission was deployed. All of that time had allowed scientists to gather volumes of data about the heavenly body, which now filled their days and nights as they attempted to understand what they would be facing.

Sadie absolutely bubbled with anticipation. Audrey was more cautious. What if they didn't land properly? What if the data, grossly outdated as it now was, was wrong? What if something had changed in the nearly seven hundred years they had been hurtling through the galaxy? What if they opened the hatch doors only to find out that they were immediately and lethally allergic to spores which floated on the soft winds greeting them with a swift death?

"What if it's perfect?" Sadie countered. "Sunshine and grass and everything you and I have ever dreamed of that isn't in this hermetically sealed air bubble in space."

As they drew closer, Sadie and Audrey began to retool things on the ship to aid them in colonization. They needed gardening tools and instruments that would analyze the native species they would discover. Luckily they had a water purifier, a matter reclaimer they could use for compost and enough nutrient paste to get them to a place of sustainability, even if gardening took several generations to master. Audrey created a tool out of some of the diagnostic equipment to look for male embryos. Among the nearly one thousand frozen Mercuries on board the ship, two dozen more were confirmed male. Enough to insure genetic diversity until the natural process took hold.

One morning, at 3:02 am Earth time, they caught sight of the planet. Larger than the home planet they had never seen, it was a swirling blue ball of oceans and tranquil cloud masses. "Isn't she beautiful?" Audrey asked, falling back into her seat.

"Perfect," Sadie sighed in agreement. "Now we just need to find a place to land."

MERCURY 23 REPORTING. We are abandoning the mission to reach the Virgo overdensity. Supplies are limited and, if the retention of human life is to be effected, the mission must be aborted. We are set to colonize Keplar 22-b, which, from here on out, will be renamed Elysium. Every attempt will be made to continue with scientific discovery and research. If the equipment survives landing, we will send back our progress. This may be the last report. Thank you, Marilla. Mercury 23 out."

Audrey switched off the com link and began the landing procedure. Moses was strapped into a safety harness that Sadie had engineered. The two women secured themselves as they began the descent. "I hope this landing gear actually works, since they never truly expected us to return," Audrey said half under her breath.

"Only one way to find out," Sadie smirked.

"Engage reverse thrusters," Audrey's voice took on the tone of a commander.

"Engaging reverse thrusters."

"Approaching thermosphere." Audrey was calmed by the task at hand. Procedure and method distracted her from thoughts of annihilation.

The ship began to shake as it descended. "Thrusters holding. Hull intact. Speed on target."

"Entering mesosphere increase reverse thrusters 20%."

"Increasing reverse thrusters." The ship vibrated through the floor and up into the seats, jarring their voices. Beneath the surface, Sadie was terrified, but her mother's cool demeanor kept her steady.

"Approaching stratosphere, it's going to get rough," Audrey warned. "Increase reverse thrusters 20%."

"Increasing thrusters. Hull intact. Fuel at 5%. We aren't going to make it."

"Adjust the angle of incline. We have room to go long."

"Adjusting. We just lost thruster four. Compensating other thrusters."

"Entering Troposphere. Give me all you have on those thrusters Sadie. Brace yourself for landing."

"Thrusters to full. Fuel at 2%." The ship was shuddering with such force that Sadie feared every piece would dislodge itself and fall away to be burned up in the atmosphere. Moses began to cry, motivating her to concentrate. "Fuel at 1%. Loss of thruster six and eight. Compensating."

"Lowering landing gear. Target in sight. Impact in five, four, three, two..."

THE DUST SETTLED like rain around the mostly intact carcass of what was once the greatest experiment man had undertaken. A trail of twisted metal gleamed in contrast to the charred path forged in the lush vegetation. Sounds of alarm could be heard as the local fauna escaped into the surrounding terrain.

The world quieted again and life resumed its usual pace, only moderately disturbed by the din of foreign matter colliding with the landscape.

The air lock opened. Audrey stepped onto burnt earth, cradling a broken arm. She took a deep breath. The air was clean, almost sweet, and she filled her lungs.

Sadie came out behind her, shading her brown eyes from the bright sun with one hand while she held Moses to nurse in the other. Her smile lit up her face and ignited Audrey's in the same gesture. She kicked off her boots and walked barefoot into the grass. "We're home, Moses," Sadie said, shining.

"Thank you Sadie." Audrey embraced her family with her obedient arm. "Now let's get to work."

Seth, the boy with two arms, would have a thousand. Not physically. Not emotionally. Not delusionally. Seth embraces the possibility of metamorphosis as hope for salvation. No Gregor Samsa, he would rejoice were he to find himself transformed. No dung beetle, the new-born millipede would be free from the burden of empathy. Seth seeks a purity unattainable by conventional human beings. Were he to awaken as Richard IV, he would never look back.

The Boy With A Thousand Arms

Ness Boers

"How are you today, Richard?"

No answer.

I didn't expect one, given that I was talking to a millipede.

Richard IV lay curled into a spiral in his tank. I knelt on the floor in front of the low table his home sat on. With Richard IV (or any of his predecessors) there was never any eye contact. It was better that way.

Richard unwound himself and crawled around the perimeter of the glass enclosure. I lifted the mesh top off of the tank and scooped the millipede up with my other hand. He squirmed a little but quickly calmed down when I set him next to a rotting strawberry.

My mother called from downstairs that it was time to go. I put on my dress shoes and left the room.

Sometimes I envied Richard.

II

We sat silently in the church pews. My mother held a handkerchief up to her eyes and whimpered slightly.

Every few minutes an extended family member (or a gang of them) would come up to us and say things like

"Oh, I'm so sorry about Christina"

or

"Are you going to be okay? You're welcome at my house any

time, dear"

They spoke to my mother as they would to a child, one too young to understand death or loss, one who still played peek-a-boo because she didn't understand object permanence.

The comforter, a baby-talking mother, the victim, a sniveling newborn - Is this what empathy reduces us to?

The distant family members coming up to us with their unneeded empathy slowed down as the day droned on. It had been quiet for a few minutes, until my aunt came up to my mother and squeezed her shoulder.

"How's Seth feeling? He must be heartbroken, the poor boy. I know he was Christina's favorite grandson."

"I'm right here," I wanted to say, but I couldn't bring myself to say anything at all.

I actually wasn't heartbroken. I felt a sort of ache in my chest, but I didn't feel like crying.

I knew they needed me to cry. So I cried. I cried for someone else for the first time I could ever remember. I had only ever cried for myself before.

Selfish? No, the state of being "selfish" was a social construct, created by humans.

Animals don't care if you're selfish. Millipedes don't care if you're selfish. To them, it's all survival. They do what has to be done.

I didn't care if people thought I was selfish. Richard didn't think I was selfish. To him, the idea of "selfishness" didn't exist.

I wish it didn't. I wish humanity didn't exist.

didn't want to be human.

III

I didn't lack empathy. Empathy is a word created by humans for humans. It's a human emotion.

I wasn't human.

I took Richard IV outside. I told him it was for fresh air. Humans would call that a lie. To me, it was only part of the truth.

People always told me I was brutally honest, to the point of fault. What reason would I have to lie? The truth was simply what was there. Nothing more, nothing less. Nothing they couldn't see for themselves.

Millipedes don't lie. Was I a millipede?

I carried Richard far from my house, across the streets, into the park. The trees towered above us. I felt like they were welcoming us. I felt at home. At that moment I wanted to run away, to live in the park forever. I wanted to crawl under a rock to hide from humanity.

Millipedes hide from their predators like that. I must be a millipede.

When we arrived in the clearing, I let Richard down. He took in his surroundings using his antennae.

I said, "Go."

Richard stayed.

I poked his back to urge him along. He began to move slowly.

I had to let Richard go. Keeping a pet was too human. I didn't want to be human. I didn't want to deal with the small talk. I didn't want to deal with the false sympathy or pretending everything was okay when it wasn't. I didn't want two arms for hugging or shaking hands.

If I had my way, I would have a thousand arms for holding myself in, a thousand arms for keeping everyone out.

Richard turned his body so his head was facing me.

I turned and walked toward my house.

Only humans look back.

The offering, "The Days of Wine and Roaches," is possibly not a true short story, at least not a conventional one. Half fiction, half non-fiction, the piece attempts to blend the two genres into a humorous comment on the sometimes surrealistic nature of real life.

Days of Wine and Roaches

James J. Slattery

Yesterday afternoon I chanced to tune my truck's Sirius radio into the opening of "Box of Rain," an elegiac composition honoring Phil Lesh's dying father, its title featuring "Box" as a stand-in for any of the other possible terms referring to that which we average, unimaginative souls might term "World." In some sort of synchronous manifestation of merest coincidence the song also stands as the last live offering of the last live performance of the Grateful Dead before Jerry Garcia's death. As some might have said were such to have happened in 1965 or even '75 rather than '95, "OH WOW!"

Now, this particular tale has little to do with rain or for that matter Phil Lesh and the Dead, at least not in its ultimate purpose; however, the song awoke in me the sleepy dawn of some sort of inspiration. Rain does not come in boxes. My early morning muse — I choose Melpomene for the ironic effect — with a bit of assistance from her sister Clio freed my mind from the bonds of attention necessary to navigating the potholes of route 4, and as the truck steered itself along its restricted little way, my imagination departed for fields never really too far removed at all. I imagined that I remembered a story, and I had. It involves a strange and hazy tale from days of Owsley Stanley and the sunshine-bright orange of the inquiring mind.

It seems the members of the band were on some sort of camping trip upon the shore of an unsilent sea when, lo and behold, what should appear but a box, wooden and abandoned.

Inside they discovered a most alive lizard. In typically humane fashion all returned to their "bus" — was it Further only they can know — whereupon Phillip fell into a most natural-seeming sleep, dreamt of those synesthetic precincts wherein only the initiated may gain admittance, and, upon awakening, there upon his very breast stretched the lizard, its breath no more, its life-force spent. The box was closed. How then, except miraculously, did the Gecko escape? But further, what greater secrets might be lying upon sea-washed shores awaiting the dawning of their new day as an unwary hand opens the lid so long confining their mystical natures? In other words, Phil wrote the music, and Robert Hunter, who wasn't even there, wrote the lyrics.

Anyway, absurd introductions finally gotten by, I was led to think how not only does rain not come in boxes, but once upon a time within the range of my three-score and ten-year memory neither did other liquids of any sort. Milk and soda came in bottles, juice in bottles or cans, and alcohol of all sorts, way, way back, came in bottles only, eventually graduating to cans, but never evolving further. To this day have you ever seen or even heard of a "box of beer," or of Pepsi... or even milk? Uh oh, milk does now come in cartons. But a box of Scotch? Really!

Then, however, just as my little truck pulled safely into our driveway, the abomination of a "Box of Joe" rose up before me, blotting out whatever straight-on vision was left. And then, from the dark heart of my memory arose a further abomination, this one of cosmic proportions. A box of wine! What the hell? Only the great deceiver, the evilest of the evil could have envisioned, let alone created a horror of such dark proportions.

Did not Pandora's Box (actually a jar as I understand it) contain all the evil of all the universe? Who do you think put all that stuff in there anyway? Is the Great Deceiver yet at work among us? Was one of his many names Thomas? Thank you Clio, the box of wine originated in 1965, the result of a malpassant inspiration of Thomas Mangove's. In truth, the vintage is held inside the box, inside a plastic envelop of sorts, not unlike a pig's bladder—or a human organ for that matter — thus eliminating the danger of cardboardiness replacing the dreaded corkiness of the bottled product. Anyway…. According to myth, Pandora's Jar also contained Hope, a comforting thought perhaps. But in a box of wine? What hope could possibly remain once the contents have been drained and then released into the world via…? You know the process.

SOME DAYS, A big old chair in our living room sits directly in the warm path of a sampling of the sun's energy upon the last few feet of its cosmic journey. There I sat, and there a fitful somnolence overtook me from which arose the following:

One otherwise uneventful Napa Valley evening, a particularly alcoholic blattarian — cockroach — scuttled her errant way across the edge of a great vat in the process of receiving a copious infusion of rosé. From a broader perspective the vat was merely a moderately sized tub, but then one must forgive the limited awareness of those counted among God's lesser creatures. Along the deliciously slippery edge did she venture until…. It may have been a gust of non-existent wind or even a gloved and mischievous hand—can anyone say—that toppled her over into the most delightful sea of dreams ever a roach set sail upon.

In no lengthy order, the process, moving inexorably toward the denouement of another story entirely, had spit the contents, including the little Periplaneta Americana into a plastic sack, and then thudded the whole thing into a dark and most comforting container of mysterious construction. Never would the roach awaken from her miraculous state of inebriation. For several days she floated in a most heavenly state of sensual deprivation. Except of course a deeply-held awareness of her intense intoxication. She needn't even wiggle her weightless legs or attempt to unfold her useless anyway wings. At first she merely bathed in the warm liquid baptism of near total immersion, but soon she came to realize, somewhere way outside of her limited self, that she was no longer afloat upon the crest of something deeper than any blattarian understanding could fathom. No! She slowly was becoming the substance, the liquor surrounding her. She was merging with the divinely intoxicating, most holy nature of life and death itself, all being and non-being, time and no-time. The grapes into wine, the roach into spirit accomplished, Hope (for that was her name) floated about in segments coming apart and drifting in that cavern measureless to man but not to cockroach, until a party of innocent women, led by their hostess Dora, drained the box over the course of an evening spent in the kitchen of a home, wherein, in another room, men, their men, snorted, howled, and stuffed their maws with salted snacks of infinite variety, chewed upon varietious pizzas, and drank beer.

Yes, beer, clear and Hopeless from.... Again you guessed it, Bottles.

"THE LYRICS COME from an old story from the band. The whole band went on a camping trip one time and they were walking on the beach. They found a small wooden box abandoned on the beach. When they opened it they found a lizard living inside it so they took it back on the bus with them. Later that day while the box with the lizard in it was left on a table on the bus Phil took a nap. He had a very strange and apparently really trippy dream that had to do with his father. When Phil woke up the lizard was dead but it was lying on his chest. Nobody knows how it got out of the box but after that happened it rained nonstop for 6 days. I did not make this up, my father was on the Dead Tour and met Jerry Garcia, Jerry told him this story."- Graham, Middletown, RI.

"Embarkation" *is the author's attempt to write a normal short story centered upon normal people. He failed.*

Embarkation

James J. Slattery

1

I walk life's miles without any shoes.
How I envy she who has no feet.
That one need not walk at all.
                    Olga Burian
                    August 1969

As her Forester slid neatly into the one vacant space outside Dunkin Donuts, Angelica fell into the most frustrating and stereotypical of her many failure oriented behaviors. As soon as she almost, with distinct emphasis upon the **almost,** completed any activity, but especially such ordinary processes as parking Subes, her attention broke free of the task at hand and like some sort of waterbug skittered off to more interesting fields of imaginative fire. So it came to pass that, as her eyes wafted up toward the rear-view mirror for a quick check of her face, the ever flawed, despite her ardent and most artful attention, public image Nature had provided, she herself floated away from the world outside the tinted glass of her crimson chariot. Her nose was not really too big, but one nostril most assuredly flared its god-awful cavern larger than the other, and was otherly shaped as well. The left one! Right one in....

Crumple, crackle, and *thud,* the Subaru slammed into the curbing, further scraping that front thing, whatever it is and

101

whatever its incomprehensible purpose, and no doubt stressing her poor, two-year old tires. Then she died. The poor baby was standard—how Angelica adored shifting, allowing Subes to roll back just a bit before perking forward when she was stopped on a hill. Somehow that made her feel just a bit larger than life, her own life at least, but circumstances such as this were totally humiliating. Angelica was far too accomplished to have allowed such a thing to happen. Once she had been stopped at a light, and the tractor–trailer just given the green had lurched, literally hopped a few feet and then shuddered to a diesel halt, stalled halfway through the intersection. Angelica knew how that driver must have felt; she felt like that herself in the present circumstances. Some of her friends called their SUV's trucks, but they were all automatic, requiring no more skill than would a car or perhaps a mini-van. Subes was no truck. But almost. She was standard shift, five speed, and Angelica could drive stick as well as any man, especially Karl. Distressed by her apparent incompetence showing itself in front of the mixture of students from her husband's college across the street, office types from down the road at the Tech Center, and, as usual, a few indecipherables and undescribables from somewhere out in a world she, thankfully, need not have any commerce with, Angelica could not escape the feeling that such blunders spoke of systemic ineptitude and a most stereotypically feminine inability to handle the complexities of shifting, steering, and braking. If they knew she had been checking out her face….

One way to avoid embarrassment is to eschew the occasion of such, and true embarrassment requires people, an audience of those who know. Thus did Angelica remain inside her parked vehicle, projecting an intense concentration upon certain matters within the folder she quickly propped against the perfectly adjusted steering wheel. A few minutes' delay would not compromise her schedule, and surreptitiously she took the opportunity to inspect the hem of her new red dress, especially purchased for that day's meeting. In his usual obsessive manner, upon her first emerging from her room into the common upstairs hallway, Karl, already "bright and chipper as spring's first expectant robin" (his tired and totally annoying imagery), noticed the flag of the type also known as an "Irish pennant." There it waved its signal for all the world to see: CHEAP DRESS! And truth be told it was not cheap. *Inexpensive!*

Angelica loved Marshall's. That store held top-of-the-line treasures, often concealed in plain sight among mere baubles, awaiting the discerning eye of the truly persistent and often just plain lucky huntress. Most fortunate, she had thought herself upon first spying the darling—no, "darling" wasn't it. It was sweet and all, but the kind of sweetness one finds in an extra dark chocolate truffle, its center liquid ecstasy of the most elemental nature. It was a dress that upon the right frame (hers) would drive both men and women wild all the while asserting its innocence, flirting a tickle bit above a most well-rounded knee, a joint, her left, with simply the tiniest beauty mark just above the larger bump of her tiny patella. No coy mistress, the red BCBG cap sleeve sheath, had blazed its "Take me. Now!" from out a jumbled-up, picked-over rack of rags too unremarkable as ever to become forgettable.

When she tried it on…. OH MY GOD! Never had she looked so good! Her hair that day had been hideous, bunched back by and escaping from a cheap CVS clip; her tan was fading, and her shoes—flip flops—decidedly did nothing for her calves and added not a millimeter to the delightful little arcs Karl so predictably termed her *derriere.* But in those glorious mirrors she, Angelica Perforce, shone truly angelic in the most profound, unholy sense that term could ever connote. She was, she knew, and would be even more so once properly bathed, made-up, *coiffed,* shod, scented, and accessorized, hot as Hell and spotless as Blake's little Lamb. With this dress, would she not effectively frame herself herself?

The morning, that morning, of the meeting came round at last, time's winged chariot having taken its maddeningly sweet time in arriving at her anxious door. Up at 5:30 she had toiled most scrupulously, showering, shaving, drying, brushing, combing, trimming, deodorizing, crying over the too blue tinge of her best black heels, making up, drawing and then redrawing her eyebrows, peeing, wiping, washing, and then changing underwear just in case. Oh, Lord, her period! It was due tomorrow. A *Light Days* wouldn't hurt. Much better safe than sorry. A final touch. Wrists and throat only, three tiny drops of her favorite scent, *Allure*, $120.00 a bottle at *Nordstrom* but worth every penny and more. Only then did she unlock the bedroom door, stepping out confidently upon three and one half inch heels into the world awaiting her debut.

Karl! He would be a complete bastard if only he were not so totally legitimate. And apologetic. And mild. And…. As she descended the stairs, Little Robin Red Breast close upon her, his mild voice sang, "Angie! Let me see a minute," and there, halfway between floors, he took her skirt in his hands, sliding it up until it bunched about her hips. Before the protest, the refusal, could issue forth, before she could twist away, he blurted. "No! Wait. There's something hanging from your hem."

The Celtic pennant it had been, a red tracing across the back of her knee he had noticed, blood upon *au lait*. Once descended to the kitchen, Karl had knelt at her backside, determined the flag to merely be a stray afterthought of some careless seamstress, and had been able to remove it with the aid of the tiny pair of scissors they kept in the junk drawer for just such occasions. For a moment then he allowed his dry hand to clasp her knees together as he brushed his lips fleetingly across the tingly flesh of their hollows. "Good luck," he had murmured, "I'll have something special for my new head writer when she gets home."

SHE WAS SO lucky to have found that man. He was a great cook, and whatever else the day might offer, a Karl meal could just possibly be the centerpiece and the capstone. He was not much in the looks department, even when a much younger man of twenty-six as he had been upon their first acquaintance at one of that impossible Olga Burian's *soirees*, the talk already grown tedious by the time he arrived, Angelica's imagination already beginning to flit about a bright field of satiric possibilities behind the cover of her fathomless black eyes and ever genuine and attentive smile. The little slut with him—for such she surely was—all long legs and micro-skirt, had been unable to keep her hands to herself: caressing his nearly feminine fingers, the fine bone of his jaw, fooling with his hair, performing little flirtations with her salmon-nailed toes, freed from their flip flops, seemingly as prehensile as a monkey's. Maybe she was able to take…. Angelica wouldn't go off to that place. She just wouldn't. Whatever could even such a skank see in the horn-rimmed geek sitting so prim and composed on the floor beside her, his long bare legs poking from the too-brief cuffs of a pair of worn jean shorts, their pockets too long for the fabric meant to contain them, those skeletal appendages somehow spidered up into a full lotus position, an expression of rapt attention frozen upon his chinless face? And the smell…. They both smelled of weed.

"Sorry to be so late," the whore, who it turned out was a biology instructor at Ithaca College, had softly projected across the room to their hostess, "but we just finished up at *La Cucina Romana*, and you do understand how it is simply impossible not to linger over an *espresso* and, of course, a cannoli."

Olga, of course, did understand, as did they all. Murmurings of imagined as well as remembered gustatory delight ebbed and flowed gently about the room for several seconds until that tide expended its limited energy, and, within their so very finite closed system, inertia once again assumed dominance over such insignificant digressions. Silence settled upon the candlelight gathering, and the glow returned to the beginning to darken countenance of Ms. Burian. "Shall we resume," she suggested rather than asked.

Their silence spoke for them all. "Of course."

They were gathered, twenty-two in all, to partake of an evening of poetry, presumably enhanced by the sacramental offering of two moderately sized, expertly constructed, marijuana cigarettes. Joints, Angelica had always called them, but the "marijuana cigarette" was Olga's term, and the lean, little fatties were Olga's fare. Anyway, they might as well have been tobacco for all the buzz that number, most of them inexpert as though they had never before gotten high, could ever hope to achieve from two stupid joints. Of course there was wine. One bottle of red, one of tepid white—something pretentious or other.... But two freaking bottles! And little bowls of trail mix or something, pretty bowls to be fair, but one horrible horrible snack. Angelica made a pact with herself to sneak out at the first opportunity. She had shown, had been noted.

No doubt there would be further refreshments after the centerpiece of the gathering—a reading of their hostess' latest work in progress, an ode to her dear and departed friend, Robert Singer, but whatever that "further" might be, Olga's poetry would have, by the time some lights came up, blunted most appetites for anything but departure. She had read Olga's work before, had sat through two of her coffeehouse readings—one at the new Café Lena, and as a minimally accomplished writer herself and holder of an MFA from Columbia, Angelica had become convinced of the absolutely pedestrian nature of her friend's imagination as well as the verse issuing from it. So it was that, as Olga scratched about herself in search of something or other, perhaps her glasses, and, as her notebook, filled to overflowing with tatters of colored paper, thumped to the floor, Angelica sidled around the corner of the archway, ducked past the indoor palm and unobtrusively made an exit through a side door out into the blackness of the driveway.

A strike. A harsh laugh. A lighter more delicate one. Shadows against a haloed streetlight, the slut and Spiderman, huddled within the glow of a match.

Out again. "Shh…shh…." Giggle…giggle…. "Who's there? Is anybody there? Olga?"

The quickening shuffle of beginning to patter feet tickled a rill of laughter from Angie. The two losers were already stoned. And paranoid. "Freeze," she giggled. "Police."

"Really?" the slut inquired. "I remember you. Didn't I see you take a hit off that mini in there? Cops aren't supposed to do that…are they?"

"She's no cop," the Karl geek pronounced. "I know her. She adjuncts at the college. English, I think." With that he fired up the number, inhaled and passed it over to Ms. Hotso.

Angelica had never seen the guy before, and she only taught one class at any college, specifically Hudson Valley Community, Freshman Composition, 6:00 to 8:50 Thursday evenings. She knew no one there except the department secretary, and spider here was no Sylvia Andrews. So where on earth had the two of them ever met?

Karl and Bertie, for that turned out to be the slutty one's "preferred handle," had paused at the curb, and Bert called back over her shoulder, "We thought we might head over to Coldstone for some ice cream. If you want, you're welcome to ride along with us."

Really? Ice cream? Having almost caught up with them, Angelica stopped just a reach away from the geek. "I'd better not," she demurred. "You know, three's a crowd and all that."

The two of them seemed to find that last hilarious. "What?" Karl choked, "You think we're a couple or something? Not in a million years, I assure you. Why, Bert's about…."

"As gay as my name might imply, you were about to say?"

"You know it, Guy," Karl guffawed, and, throwing his arms about her and she hers about him, the two careened about the front lawn eventually throwing themselves down in a neighbor's front yard in a quivering heap of some sort or other of entangled gender confusion.

Angelica knew not at all what to do or say, and so took the most logical of all possible paths. Straight toward her car.

"Wait," the two called together. "Come on with us. We'll explain everything."

"TRY THIS, BERT had demanded, thrusting a fragrant pipe of sweet smelling ganja at her. "Coldstone's best enjoyed while way, way under the influence."

What was she doing? Crushed between the two of them in the front seat of some tiny car of some obscure make, she could not have explained straight, and after that first hit, no explanations were possible, nor were they necessary. Things had become what they were, and that was all she needed to know. They were in the creamery. She knew not what she had ordered, but it was minty and chocolately with some peanutbutter essence somewhere at its heart. Nothing had ever been that good and nothing ever would be again. Or so Angie thought.

The two explained themselves, and later she would find she almost remembered it as they had revealed it, and they had almost revealed themselves and their relationship as it truly was. Ever must there be secrets, always an alternative to the perceived reality must be allowed to exist, but for the most part their relationship was simple: lonely, geeky guy keeps company with lonely, sexy lesbian who has no time for romance of any sort but the most casual and impersonal. The Nerds at Ithaca would have resigned their PhD's for a night with Bertie, and some of the more persistent had become more than mere annoyances. So did it flare into existence: boyfriend/girlfriend, Karl and Bert. They didn't elaborate, but Angelica surmised the caresses were not all act. How far that sort of thing went, she never asked, but as she came to know them better, she suspected Bert, without compromising either her principles or her devoutly cherished orientation, had found ways to please Karl and that Karl not only shielded her from unwelcome attention but also provided a certain warmth and comfort at the very least approaching an acceptable variety, eccentric and improvisational as it might be, of the love all humans long for. While not a couple at all then, they had become a most happy duet, their song not strange but haunting, sweet and profoundly sad. As they sat in the garish light, the world dark and strange about them, amid the discordant chattering of too many enthusiastic creamers, Karl's and Angie's eyes met in all their shared stoned vulnerability, and their marriage procession began.

Bert remained a friend. Had once made the inevitable suggestion, and upon refusal had smiled, nodded acceptance, and had slowly faded into the years as a Christmas card, birthday call friend, several hundred lineal miles, and leagues upon emotional and social leagues removed from Angelica's and Karl's chosen life.

ANGELICA KNEW THAT everything about her, including the hem of her dress, was as absolutely perfect as anything can ever be; she also knew nobody at all cared how she maneuvered and parked her car... but.... In her imagination there was always another. Not Karl, not her mother or father, not anyone with a face or physical presence. She sometimes thought the presence was she herself. But a philosophy? Or was it psychology? course had instilled into her conscious mind the very limiting concept of the indisputable necessity of object and observer possessing separate identities. She was herself; *ergo* (must have been philosophy), were she being observed, of necessity the observer was a distinct and separate *other*. But who or what? Berkley (definitely philosophy) no doubt would have said "God," and *Monsignor* Knox would have agreed. If God gives a peek and a thought to trees, then why not to the numerous complexities comprising the everyday existence of the modern American woman? Or man, for that matter? Most troubling though is that concept for her who dwells astraddle the border between profound agnosticism and absolute atheism. If there is no god, and if she is incapable of observing herself, then who might the watcher or watchers be? Like any good MFA, Angelica relegated that question to sleepless nights when any thought at all becomes compulsive, when endless possibilities arise from the most elemental of matters. No wonder so many of her contemporaries had turned to some variety of faith—not the traditional deceptions, obviously, but such novelties (for them only) as some mild form of Zen, Tibetan Buddhism, environmentalism, animal rescue, tiger moming, bicycling, marathoning, adventureering, or any of the other myriad facets of that most alluring middle-class American focus upon fitness, both psychological and physical. Angelica long ago had chosen education, interesting and rewarding employment, writing, and her own mirror. She could see herself as an other in each and collectively all of those areas of her life. Often, humans, especially women, are far more complex and capable than either philosophers or psychologists (for too long, mostly men) have ever seemed able to recognize or, if recognized, to comprehend. She absolutely was capable of observing herself. Perhaps not accurately…hmm…. She would have to think that one through.

IF ONLY SHE could somehow become so hopelessly lost in thought that she would for ever after find herself unable to return to the inauthentic fabric of the car seat, the unpleasant bulk of the Light Days bunched up down there where monthly she bled, the dirty parking lot, the bus-fouled atmosphere of the roadside, and of course the painful din of all the ignoranti slogging about their jobs, their pathetic cravings for caffeine, fat, and calories inside the bright confines of the coffee scented Vandenburg Avenue Dunkin Donuts. That she was one of them she need not be reminded, upon her own holey quest for a dozen donuts and a Box O' Joe along with the accompanying lactic and sacchric toxins so necessary to render the bitter brew potable. Standing in line, "on line," they said in the city, and that was her preferred preposition; somehow "on" seemed less confining than "in," thereby allowing one to feel removed from the gluteus masses around her....

She was third from the counter, crammed up against the plastic topped post stretching its brown belt off toward another of its awful kind... and she didn't even remember coming in. Had she turned Subes off...? Yes, she had her keys.... Had she locked her...? Too late.... She really had been removed, not hopelessly lost in thought perhaps, but for a blessed time free of the oppressive bulk of reality, which, like some obese lover pressing its will upon her, intruding upon every possible opening her too vulnerable self unwillingly yet defenselessly offered up to the world, too soon again smothered her within the overlapping folds of its importunity, stifled all her possibilities save the imagination—her only escape. But, here she was: about to order coffee and tasteless snacks for her staff at the paper—all of them impossible egos as would be any group of arts, food, and entertainment writers. To top it off, she had come from outside, having been a free-lancer at Metroland and occasional feature writer for the Times Union, until this very Monday that is. Today she assumed the role of Arts and Entertainment Editor of the daily edition as well as Editor of the Sunday *Unwind* and *Travel* sections. Karl insisted upon calling her Head Writer, probably due to his devotion to the old Dick van Dyke Show. Would that she could move them to Westchester and find herself head writer of SNL. Fat chance though, at least for now.... Maybe Walter Mitty!

She had almost laughed out loud. What sort of spectacle would that have been?

The line moved; she had become second. Who might have assumed her old, her odd place in this new reality? Who really cared? No longer willing to risk reaccessing her "dream world" as her mother—and her sixth-grade teacher—had called it and expose herself to the ridicule such public excursions sometimes precipitated, Angelica concentrated instead upon the pleasant tension produced in her calves by her shoes, especially when she cocked one ankle so that her front foot balanced upon the tip of its heel and she could observe her pointed little toe waggle playfully back and forth. Reality wasn't all bad she soon realized, especially when she was able to direct her attention, as she was doing, away from the seedier aspects of the otherness all around.

PERHAPS IT WAS the smell of diesel from a passing bus; whatever it was, just as she settled her weight upon both feet and prepared to take her place at the counter, she felt it, the hem of her skirt being raised, not gently, respectfully, with naught but benign intent as Karl had done that morning, but roughly, the force most urgent, and bordering upon violent, its lascivious purpose most abundantly clear. A darkness loomed behind her, its inhuman breath forbidding even the slightest taste of unfouled air. Into her mind it did creep, the paranoia of the defenseless prey just fallen beneath the shadow of the circling raptor, the hawk most actual, thereby rendering the paranoia most unreal as is any purely imaginary mental state. An other's talons held her; she felt its cold breath, trembling, awaited the thrust of its....

It was no bird. Just a man. But what sort of man was he? He was inside her most completely. Not her mere physicality. Her mind...her total awareness. She saw herself...from behind, from his perspective but with her own perceptions, her own eyes. His thoughts muttered in the background; his desire ebbed and flowed randomly yet somehow purposefully as well.

Oh how cute! The six black buttons stitched in light, blue-grey vertically upon each side of the black, waist-length leather jacket she so ecstatically had commandeered right off a mannequin at Macy's. The only one of its kind in the entire store. Yes, it had cost more than just the proverbial arm and a leg, but it was so soft, and now, there on line in Dunkin Donuts, a rapist at her heels, Angelica realized for the first time that it must have been tailored with her exact shape in mind if not somehow created especially for her and only her. Someday she might write a story dedicated to this moment and her awareness of the perfection she had somehow chanced upon in the Colonie Center Mall. *Angelica's Jacket* she should call it....

The muttering of the unseen presence intensified until it seemed the other patrons must hear. The beast was poised; like a cat at her time, Angelica could only cower before his need; trembling both with fear and her own desire, she could not resist the hands as they worked her skirt up to immodest heights, as harsh breath tore to shredded black-leather pennants the rationality of her frantic consciousness. As Joyce might have written, she would swoon—she adored that word. Joyce not quite so much—into the snowbright darkness of this delicate moment and succumb to the fury upon her.

"Ma'am? ...Ma'am? May I help you, Ma'am?" She was next. The mocha toned fat man in D.D. brown and pumpkin appeared anxious, possibly just a bit concerned. His voice and posture, however, remained unruffled. She felt a conjecture, "Must have got hers really good last night," flit through his mind, but she knew his only true vision was of loneliness, and the slow drone of hours the only song of all his livelong days. Any further awareness of the counterman's sad reality inaccessible to her, Angelica jolted back into that limited coexistence into which they had by circumstances so casually been thrust. She knew she looked and felt foolish, that her voice would quickly betray her confusion. High-pitched and squeaky, it would shrill out its pathetic sentences into the tumbling cadences of those more pleasantly modulated conversations around her. *Pathetic!*

"Not at all," quoth the dark one from behind.

Abruptly, she ordered, wasting no time on the donuts. This meeting would rely on coffee alone; donuts were an extravagance anyway; besides, they were super fattening.

"The muffins more so," interjected he who perched behind.

She just had to get a look at him.

"You..." he began.

Cutting him short, Angelica spun upon her heels as though they were track shoes, the words of confrontation geysering forth. "Just who in hell do you think...."

No one was there; nothing but the shadow of a passing truck.

"Mam?" issued from behind, "Mam... will there be anything else?"

"No, thank you," baaed from her wooly throat as she presented the man with a twenty dollar bill, almost forgetting her change, actually forgetting to tip, "I'll wait over here (indicating a seat by the window). Call me when my order is ready. Please."

2

Too fat to be more than hungry,
Too down to ever get up,
Too dead even to die,
I weep that I am I.
> *Olga Burian,*
> *April 2009*

All the short road home, Angelica mulled over the day, uncharacteristically failing to recognize, let alone become immersed as she ordinarily might have, in her new favorite song as it played itself out unnoticed through Subes' less than stellar system. Foster the People's *Pumped Up Kicks* might be just a trifle out of place amid the mild vibrations of a Subaru purring along I-787 bearing its passenger home to a fine surprise meal and whatever other delights await an expectant woman returning home from an absolutely first-rate day at her marvelous new job, but had Angie not been so completely distracted by the myriad of glittering impressions, like kittens crowding each other away from the silver dish of her consciousness, she most certainly might have chosen to tune it out anyway. The afternoon, not yet even begun to hint at fading, was blessed by the beneficent sunlight of early September and a warm breeze teased at her hair through the partially lowered window. Life was surely good. Perhaps it could get no better.... *Now, now, just say no to darkness*, and Angie smiled all the way home into their newly sealed driveway before any thoughts other than pleasant ones returned.

Right there, as blatant as a slap in the face, piled the intestinal leavings of that idiot's dog. Her neighbor! Supposed neighbor anyway. She'd definitely have to have Karl say something.... If she were to confront the imbecile, there would be no telling what might occur. She was a bit extreme, Angie realized, and a realistic, firm approach, neighborly in its own way, was needed here.

Sometimes though, there is no need for unpleasantness at all, even of the neighborly variety. Just as she stood completely free from Subes, just as her nose, one nostril larger than the other, began to wrinkle into a particularly adorable expression of distaste, the Ginger Man as she and Karl had named the scrawny, freckle-faced twerp next door, came running out with plastic bags and an apology,

"His name's Rex," Angelica laughed upon first entering the warm, earth-toned front hallway. "Rex Lancaster. God! What were his parents thinking?"

Karl, who had been observing the non-confrontational confrontation from a front window, giggled hysterically, turned and fled toward the kitchen from which whispered hints of a most delicious meal in the final stages of preparation. "Don't come out here," he commanded. "Just have a seat; you'll find a Tangueray and Tonic, cold and anxious for your approval. The New Yorker's there too. It came really early this week. Please, no TV though. OK? As Wordsworth so prosaically said, *The world is too much with us*, so let us not further lay waste our powers this day. *Pandora* would be acceptable though.... Whatever you like... just not too loud if you wouldn't mind," and with a clash and a rattle Karl disappeared into the mists of his own creation.

She loved Pandora; she could find anything there, so this afternoon, Karl in one of his "bustling moods," Angelica tapped onto one of the classical modes. Of course, the sound was perfectly modulated by their state-of-the-art home theater system, and a Bach concerto for Cello—in G Major she thought—soothed its elite strains into the quotidian clatter of their Pond Hill environment. Somewhere a mower had been humming its lethal summer recessional; across the way a dog joined its rough voice to the high glee of children at play. And then there was Karl; his kitchen spilled a happy chatter all about their cozy little home. This piece, although seemingly perfect for the occasion, mild and accepting of all the lesser melodies about it, and of course the work of the unparalleled Maestro, nevertheless, brewed up a bitches' potion dark and bottomless. Angelica hated the cello. Her parents, she would swear in any court upon any holy book in any land, had wanted her plain, fat and acne bedeviled, nerdishly studious, too good for the others around her, too unremarkable for them to care. To that end Mom and Dad had thrust the cello upon her as the instrument of their grand design. She had refused; oh yes, they had literally locked her up in the modest little cubby they so immodestly termed their studio, demanding practice,

practice, practice.... All that practice, however, she never allowed to make her perfect, and by ninth grade when she went off to Emma Willard, they had given up on the music. But not on creating the little dweeb they had thought she should for some inexplicable reason or other wish to become.

To their dismay, Emma Willard was her salvation—in the strictest, most secular sense of that word. There she had met brilliant young women from all over, not just the United States but from the far reaches of the entire world. The instruction—no the teaching—the education—had been unparalleled, and, before she knew it, Angelica had developed a sense of style, a commanding presence, and a deep ambition to become the most modern of female persons. An Emma graduate, Jane Fonda, had said it all in her 1989, commencement address, just the year before Angelica had begun her transformation at the academy, "See yourselves as an army of 96," she had urged, "women with a mission. Whether you become teachers, scientists, lawyers, urban planners, economists, actresses or housewives, you will have a role to play." Jane was and always had been more than just an actress; she had gotten herself in trouble during Vietnam, that was true, but had come out of it with character enhanced and dignity unquestioned. Most of all, her intelligence, her talent and fervor in no wise disqualified her from being devastatingly beautiful. How Angelica wished she could have been there for the address.... She had, nonetheless, taken Fonda's words to heart and had done her best within the parameters of her own talents and academic/professional ambitions.

Jane had attended Vassar; Angelica chose Bryn Mawr. Jane had pursued acting—a natural—Angelica writing. Jane had achieved great success and worldwide renown. Angelica.... Well.... Angelica had just become the newly established editor of a minor section of a minor local paper. Abruptly she switched away the annoying cello and landed upon a Nick Cave module. Thank god:

just beginning were Foster the People with *Pumped Up Kicks*.

Once in Willard, away from Them, a new member of a new and ideal sisterhood, Angelica had abandoned whatever timid impulses toward rebellion she may have harbored and had found belonging not to be all that many claimed it to be. Not **merely** all. More! Even now—Post Emma--she still belonged, had actually expanded her community beyond the limited sisterhood of adolescence into a more global reality. She and Karl were a family, their relationship both enlightened and equal. As pretentious as some of them were, she also belonged to several societies dedicated to the arts including The Albany Symphony Conductor's Circle, Friends of Chamber Music—never mind the presence of the Cello— and the successor to the Rensselaer County Council For The Arts (RCCA), *The Arts Center*. All had proven vital to the resurgence of the once blighted city of Troy, to the county, even to the state itself; indeed, the furthering of the creative side of the culture was perhaps the one most essential task any individual as part of any group might undertake. At least personally significant, as limited in scope and overall import as such might be, were her involvements with the Emma Willard, Bryn Mawr, and Columbia Alumnae Associations, and the networking possibilities already unfolding as the result of her new position at the paper stretched beyond imagining. A Pulitzer was not an unrealistic hope. Others from the TU had gone there, and she had the tools and the ambition to join that (Should she even think it?) *elite* company.

So why the fixation upon *Pumped Up Kicks*? She even had to ask someone just what pumped up kicks were. Idiotically engineered, faddish footwear for god's sake. Why would she, a lover of Bach and a Friend of Chamber Music, even tolerate such simplistic musical stylings, and how could an MFA become ensnared by violent, arrhythmic lyrics properly ignored by all but the most lowbrow? So adolescently antisocial! So contrary to all she had sometimes painfully, yet always gratefully, learned to cherish. But there she sat, shuddering with some sort of delight as the fictional Robert wielded his gun, warning all the others around him—all those who belonged, all the kids in their "Pumped up Kicks"—that death loomed over them, spreading its black wings, negating any hope of any future save that of a world wherein they no longer dwelt.

How she could go on, she chuckled. Her musings though did have some validity. She despised violence. No doubt the lyricist, if not all the members of the band, had been bullied, and the song was merely some teenage revenge fantasy set to... really, really great music. Music that touched her. And lyrics, basic and clichéd and repetitive as they were, somewhere way down deep in the pelvic bottom of her gut—*why that word gut?* She hated that word—moved her. No, she did not long for an actual gun. But a metaphorical one? Interesting... appealing. Who would she use it on though? She hated no one. Resented no one...well maybe Mom and Dad...and Dr. Foster...her only B at Columbia. *Maybe the name? Probably not.*

Such musings could go on forever and without restraint would most certainly introduce an unwelcome emotional overlay to what yet had all the promise of a most pleasant evening. As if on cue the deceptive chant of *Pumped Up Kicks* bounced its way into silence. Immediately though a possibly more dangerous offering moved through the not so desert ether, triggering memories she had forgotten were hers. Her long, not-blonde hair flyin' in Neil Young's sun, Angelica rode back unwillingly into a 1992 sixteen-year-old fantasy. She could, would ride a motorcycle, maybe not a Harley, but maybe so, across the country, across all the continents of all the world if she so wished. Her parents be darned, one thing Emma and her personification Jane Fonda had taught and were still teaching was that our possibilities are limited only by our self-imposed list of impossibilities. Then in her senior year, not yet eighteen, the crushing enlightenment of Simone de

Beauvoir's writings, especially *The Ethics of Ambiguity*, had descended upon her, for a time reducing her life's quest to a singular obsession. Somehow, in some uniquely personal way, Angelica had resolved to become one of the truly ethical individuals, perhaps mired in the same swill as the multitudes, but never of them...a woman such as Jane, as no doubt had been Emma herself. DeBeauvoir, no doubt Sartre's wellspring of imagination as well as his intellectuality, may have moved her famous husband beyond his facticities; that, however, was subject to discussion, but Simone most assuredly had never been bound up in the things and imagined titles and restrictions we allow the world and ourselves to impose upon our humanity. Even the girl on the Harley somehow represents merely a change of facticity, a set of conditions somehow more appealing than single mother, waitress, fading flower of young womanhood, young girl dreams.... Neil Young presented his waitress as sad, unfulfilled yet filled. With longing. Never, had resolved the teen angel, would she allow herself to fall so far. Never! She could both belong and remain free. Simone had, and so could she.

As must all things, her reverie might have passed softly into the next song, *If Not For You*, bittersweet for certain, but somehow always hopeful, had not Karl chosen the exact moment of Neil's mournful "Lookin' for a magic kiss." Her husband, a necessary facticity of that which she had become, a married woman, disguised as a separate and independent entity defined as Karl, arrived with a cheerful smile, a light step and a perfectly set shrimp cocktail, its arrangement copied from an upscale web site she would wager. Four ultra-jumbo shrimp, perfectly chilled, neither watery nor ice-rimed, pink tails laid upon a bed of arugula, fanned about a miniature crystal cup filled, never to overflowing, with a hot sauce so far from generic that such a common term as "hot sauce" did it no justice at all. Yes, there were tomato, horseradish, garlic, lemon, maybe basil, and another mystery or two, maybe

Worcestershire, he would not share, even with her. Whatever it was though, its facticities added up to one one-of-a-kind delicacy. "Careful," he cautioned, "we're a bit hotter than usual today."

Such was his not so subtle gambit, Angelica knew, in the game he loved to make of seduction. She would taste the shrimp before deciding how to play. He had parked himself before her, awaiting just that move. So she delayed until, frustrated, he paddled back into the kitchen.

Whatever Karl's motives might have been, his shrimp was no mere ploy. That had always been his way, to disguise the utmost insincerity within absolute sincerity or vice-versa, and as had happened on more than one occasion, even he could not always say precisely what his motives were, finding himself quite unable to be certain of the desired end of his convoluted strategies. This afternoon, at least, his approach seemed clear. "Wine and Dine and then make time," he termed it, his adolescent sense of humor covering for the often sad desperation of his emotional dysfunctions. Well, wine and dine they would, but as Joyce had put it, she was due to have her "roses," and neither she nor Karl found such blooming attractive. So, maybe just wine and dine.... She would make it up to him another day, and the dear man was ever so understanding. Perhaps the flow would hold back.... They would see.

"I think I'll go up and change into something more comfortable," she tossed.

"Please, don't," urgency speedballed back, followed closely by Karl, dress pants flopping about his thin, sockless ankles, white shirt half buttoned and hanging out over his left hip. "I want you just as you are... please, and I'm dressing too. This is, after all, a celebration not just for some journalist, but for an editor. I do believe... don't you... that a modicum of formality... elegance... might be called for?"

Maybe so, but then Angelica in a great dress and heels was

one of his turn-on's. His motives way too clear, Angelica felt a bit disappointed. Why was he not trying any harder to disguise, to misdirect, to wend with her the wicked, twisted path of seduction?

"I thought afterward," he offered, a tiny bit of hesitancy creeping into his voice, "we could go down to the Music Hall." A smile broke across all the doubtful panes of his face, excitement sweeping all the doubt from his voice. "I've been holding something back from you.... Do you know who's there tonight?" Without awaiting a reply, he blurted, "Joan Baez, that's who. And I have second row center tickets. Also," he was nearly breathless, "I emailed Marva Connors, and she may be able to convince Joan to mention you and your new job from the stage. For certain, we'll have a chance to say hello after the show."

Were she to say she was stunned, Angelica would have felt that somehow she had failed to capture the moment. All her education, all those descriptive words and phrases she had read and written over the years, and "stunned" was the best she could do? So, she said nothing, instead allowed a smile through the veil of her tears to speak for her heart. Joan Baez was a hero, perhaps the only other equal to Jane Fonda in her pantheon, and this night of this impossibly gratifying day she was going to a concert, one, regretfully, she had been too busy to remember to purchase tickets for until too late; now though, she not only would attend the show, but perhaps... just maybe... an interview? Thank you, Karl! Thank you, thank you thank....

Her roses would not this evening blossom, could not....

3

The pale cat purrs
in december twilight
in the fading light
my patchwork blurred

James J. Slattery

by the mist of
green tea rising
no more can I
but tell the hours

> *Olga Burian*
> *December 31, 2011*

The concert had been nothing short of phenomenal. Baez' voice had perhaps lost a bit of range, but the underlayment of pain and triumph, the continued hope in the face of all opposition, disappointment, and def.... No! That was it. Never had Joan been defeated. At her age, after the many years, the decades really, she yet hoped for better times, for sanity and love. Her closing number, the everlasting legacy of John Lennon, *Imagine*, said it best for Angelica, for the singer, for all of them. "Imagine all the people...."

The evening had darkened a bit though just prior to the show. In the lobby, bright lights already fading to concert intensity, Angelica had spotted another Angie, Angelina Rivera. From the *TU*. Had Angelica not been editor, this might have been her show to review, but now it belonged to that other Angie. And so too, damn it all, did any possible interview. That was exactly how it all came down. Angelica did get to say hello, but there had been no mention of her from the stage. Angelina gladly accepted the opportunity for a one-on-one, and the last Angelica saw of Joan was her back-side as she ambled down the hall with the no doubt clueless critic, all of twenty-two and probably ignorant as to the true stature of the little woman alongside whom she so confidently walked.

By the time they had gotten back to Pond Hill, Angelica, although not fully desirous of, found herself to be sufficiently consensual to the "wine and dine" climactic scene. She was really tired, and as she slipped from Karl's initial advance, ducking his tentative attempt at osculation, simply sagged onto their *Ricardo* sectional, slipping emotionally as well as physically into its ashen embrace. "Just do it," she sighed with the slightest hint of the drama he loved so much, and, hooking her thumbs into the elastic of her hipsters, she had slid them to her knees before the rosy dawn announced its presence. Thereby, she was spared his sometimes tiresome attentions. Thank you someone or other, she could just drift off to sleep, a mostly satisfying day concluding in an amusing, if awkward, finale. Good night, Karl... and you too Moon. Angelica slept, and Karl.... Karl, as often he did, took care of himself.

TO SLEEP IS always *perchance* to dream. Sometimes no dreams come. Such had been that night for Angelica, so when she awoke somewhere in the neighborhood of 5:00 AM, unhappily aware that her 5:45 alarm set made any true return to oblivion impossible, all she could force herself to do was curse the stains on her white linen, the throbbing in her back, the cramps destined to torment her all day. She would take some *Excedrin Extra Strength* and start the coffee before returning to strip her bed, start a wash, shower, etc, etc. With that in mind, she began her descent of the curved staircase the envy of all those she knew. Half the way down, however, a sulfurous cloud of some imaginative essence curled its predatory self about her, and Angelica drifted to a halt, slumped to the elegant black walnut treads swept up in the midst of a most graceful turn. The one from yesterday morning had returned. No longer was he, as she had assumed his gender to be, behind her; instead, again he was within her in a way no man had ever been.

"I am you," the no longer he hissed in a voice like unto, yet in its sibilance unlike any Jane/Joan Fonda/Baez utterance ever recorded. How does one resist one's self? Never had Angelica asked that question, and the time for such exercises was past. Thus did she allow herself to fade into a willing captivity, allowing the dark one to have her way.

Along with the cello, Angelica's parents had attempted to foist their Roman Catholic religion upon her: St. Agnes Elementary, Sunday Mass, "Bless us, O'Lord..." before evening meals, and just as she had the cello, Angelica had tossed that particular set of beliefs and practices into her own hazardous waste bin as soon as Emma had set her free. Since then, thank you William, she had diligently ignored any and all intimations of immortality. Her life was hers to live; Jane and Joan were far superior as role models than were a comically virginal mother and an oppressively male-imagined hierarchy consisting of god, son of god, boy apostles, saints, Halloweendressup churchmen, fathers and sons. Angelica had herself to create by herself, and had done a not unremarkable job of same. Yet there she sagged, her blood unstanched, will subsumed, a dark presence speaking schizophrenic tongues in her mind.

"I bleed with you," the voice whispered, "and I cry with you, laugh with you. Despair with you. Yes, despair, for you are nothing, have nothing." Laughter bounced about, cruel heat-lightning flashes of scorn. "The beauty you so prize will fade, and as soon as tomorrow will turn to maculate old age; the day after that will find your imperfectly preserved corpse rotting slowly in the cold depths of the grave, and the day after.... Nothing! Your life's energy.... Nothing! Your accomplishments.... Forgotten! Worse than worthless. Pathetic deceptions. And your much prized education? An inconsequential diversion. Your intellect.... Not at all that which it tells you it is."

Angelica, no weakling, roused herself at least to a less submissive posture, discovered in the interior gloom a spark of resistance. Clichés. The foolish presence was attempting to seduce or defeat her with some of the most vapid of freshman-level intellectual insecurities. Such required merely a sophomoric, existential response. "Resist," she shouted into the cavern of the other. "I have always resisted, and I yet say, 'No.'"

Laughter !

"And you? I have no time for you. I have coffee to make, laundry to do, and a newspaper to create. I have myself to create as well. If you are as you say, I, Myself, then have I not created you? And are you not subject to my will? I think that you are. Now go away."

Laughter.

"Camus would have found you amusing. You know that, don't you? I'm not sure, but I don't think he identified your type of suicide; he no doubt would have recognized your pathetic impulse. Perhaps he would have found you a bit player in the absurd game of philosophical denial, a hanger on, perhaps in the stale cells of Heidegger and Husserl, who, unlike Kierkegaard, can not even recognize the allure of the comforting leap into the free-fall of the abyss, who comically walks blindly in line as if part of the Peasant's satirical comment on Christ the existentialist's words, blithely unaware of the fall yet to come. No Icarus, you, or should I say 'we? You have no wings. You think you need them not. Your sun is just another aspect of an uncloudy day.

"You truly know better though. Look you, Angelica, you of many other possible names, to that which lies before you. The scales upon your eyes are of your own construction. There is no light save darkness shall ever remove them. All but a few others straggle along in the line. All but a few will fall forever unaware of the spirit within them. You have been blessed, knocked off your ass so to speak. Close your eyes. Return to your room, close the drapes, draw the blankets about your head and see."

Angelica found that all her vitality had returned. The emerging sunlight through the fan-window of the foyer needled her eyes, and, reflexively almost, she followed the dark one's instruction. At least the very first part of it. The rest though? No thank you. Instead, she stripped the bed, then herself, and showered. She

126

would catch a cup of coffee at Starbucks, French Roast, and head into work a bit early. Dark things, scales and blind men be damned. She had always preferred the light of reason to any chaotic, fanciful philosophies and theories no matter how well expressed. Perhaps there is no god; imagine there is no heaven; just the same, all was quite all right with Angelica's world.

With that thought, again fell the shadow. "You cannot escape yourself," she pronounced. "I have passively observed all you have done and failed to do. Believe me, I admire our sense of style and am proud of our intellectual accomplishments. But hating the cello? Really! However, that's just a minor aberration, one we might ignore with no significant consequences, but this new job....

"All the cliché ridden commencement addresses of your substantial academic career have addressed the theme of 'embarking' upon some sort of marvelous journey or adventure, all the possibilities of life ahead awaiting the graduate's arrival, offering their rewards to the one who dares to strive, who meets the challenges of life. Whether as one of an army of 96 or 996 matters not a whit, success is the goal; it is most desirable, and it is achievable. One truly may become all that she can be. At this point, Angelica, do we stand. You think we have made our choice and have arrived at another point of embarkation. Indeed, we have. For the first time though, your choice may lead you away from that which you might best become.

"Whatever it is you ultimately do, I will not change; I will fall silent though. Always will I be you, but a you other than the you you think you are. I know you; I see you from every possible angle in every possible sense; I am the shredded skin of your compulsive exfoliations, the light in your eyes, the love in your heart.... But even more am I that impulse which moves Mr. Foster's Robert. I would have us get our metaphorical gun and wipe away the things around us, would embark upon a most violent collision with the very air we breathe. We have talents recognized but submerged within the algaeic pool of society's expectations. You have abandoned any hope of writing or of true enlightenment. You have failed to recognize the absurdity of all you seek. Angelica, I observe your failure as one who might have become truly human. It is not too late!

"Do you remember your class in Indian philosophy? The Upanishads? The long and sometimes laborious discussions with classmates who seemed constitutionally incapable of accepting the concept of enlightenment let alone possibly seeking and achieving any sort of recognition of their true nature as human beings? And do you recall how awakened you thought you had become and how you had determined to seek your own true essence? You knew, as did Camus and other Western thinkers as well, that most, at the time you included, are ignorant of their own truth and that as such are doomed to lives of pain and futility.

"You are an exceptional human being, Angelica. And I am that which you must seek. This last time only will I attempt to change your course, to guide you. Any more is not for me to do. All I have to offer has now been given. Even if I knew for certain the way you must take to find me again, I, for your sake, would not reveal it. I am not enlightenment, but I am your true nature.

"Perhaps we shall meet again; perhaps the road you take will forever keep us apart."

AT THE END of the week, Angelica offered her 30 day notice. By the end of the year, she and Karl were divorced. She never bought a Harley Davidson, but she did learn to love the cello. Where Angie now has gone, as Emmylou Harris sings of another displaced soul flown far from his place of origin, "ain't nobody knows."

4

Requiem for an Angel

my cats come in on little fogfeet
mewing their songs each to each
so sad they never sing to me
Olga Burian
June 2013

RECESSIONAL

Angie sits in a little chair
A little smile on her little face
A little bow in her short brown hair

Outside, a bus, a car, a plane
The far off hoot of a far off train

Angie sits in a great big chair
A great big frown on her great big face
No bow at all in her permed grey hair

Outside, the sun, the moon, a star
Inside of Angie, all things too far

Angelica Perforce *nee* don Nadie
12/12/12

"The Short Plank Jig" is a tale of a retired Army captain whose son is dead, whose marriage is dysfunctional, and whose retirement is anything but satisfying. Irony is the dominant tone. Bitter irony. As one who, while serving had "helped more than a few soldiers get their heads straight," Timmons Wainwright is singularly unable to do the same for himself. Bitter, suicidal, and homicidal, Captain Wainwright seeks employment at Blythewood School, but his interview with supervisor Mike McDonald leads to his application being rejected. From this a mix of fanciful and actual interactions with Mr. McDonald occurs. At the end, the unexpected happens, and Timmons Wainwright is left both with a new job and an overwhelming question.

The Short Plank Jig

Stephen Slattery

Captain Timmons Wainwright sat on a stool in the Bamberg Officers' Club. Motionless on his perch, he stared at a double shot of Ron Rico 151. His dress blue jacket was unbuttoned and his tie skewed to the left. His carefully trimmed sandy-colored hair, always neat, was slightly mussed as if a stay finger of dry air had gently flicked it without him noticing. In nineteen years of US Army spit and polish this was the most unkempt condition in which he had ever appeared. Not that it mattered. He wasn't in the Army anymore.

After so many years of keeping everything tight, keeping everything together, it seemed impossible it was... *over.* There were many things he'd seen and disliked during his career: incompetent behavior and incompetent orders issued by incompetent officers whose professional fortunes sometimes flourished at the expense of better men. But he had always loved the Army, loved the discipline, the camaraderie — the protection it gave him from the past and the present. No human institution was perfect or above reproach, but to him the United States Army came close. As an infantry officer turned counselor, he'd helped more than a few soldiers get their heads straight and turn not just their careers but their lives around. He was proud of that.

Wainwright took a moment to survey familiar surroundings. There was talk of converting this place into some kind of conference center. Wainwright wagged his head and made a sour face. Couldn't they leave things alone? No more officers' club. The

131

democratization of the military. How far would they go? Private Jones wants to be general today. Sure. Why not?

Stupid, stupid, stupid.

Wainwright wagered his eyeteeth there was no casual fraternization between officers and enlisted men when Bamberg was the Wehrmacht's Warner Kaserne.

He idly fingered a bright brass button and looked down at his right shoulder board. Soon the uniform would disappear into a closet and he'd be back in civvies for the first time since he quit teaching public school at twenty-eight and joined the service. It was a big leap back then — brave, really.

And all for nothing .

Nineteen years, not twenty. That was too bad. But after what happened to the boy, and with the wife demanding to go back to the States, there hadn't been many choices left him — and when the Army notified him he would have to retire or be rifted back to NCO status, there were none. His professional pride couldn't take any more direct hits.

Back to Massachusetts. Home. Get a teaching certificate again. Undisciplined snot-nosed punks and a daily ration of shit.

No. Not that. He and the wife needed time to put things in perspective and back together. Breathe easy for a while.

Captain Timmons Wainwright (soon-to-be-retired) lifted the shot glass and gulped rum. His stomach twitched when the hellfire missile hit it. He lowered his chin, fighting the urge to gag. He squeezed his eyes closed only to have them pop open again as something big and ugly, not the rum, surged up from deep in his belly.

"Cocksucking Bitch!" He bellowed so loud everyone in the OC stopped talking and looked at him.

Why did I do that? he wondered. Aloud, "Excuse me, gentleman. I bit… I bit my tongue."

THE CLOCK ON the dresser was a fine Linden Triple Chime. It played three melodies: Westminster, Whittington, and St. Michaels. The chime rods were brass, clean shiny brass, and produced the most wonderful melodic notes, thirty-two of them to be exact. Wainwright bought it in Germany for the wife the Christmas before the son....

How many minutes and domestic minuets had it ticked off since then? Seven years worth and then some.

Wainwright sat naked on the edge of the bed. He looked at himself in the full-length mirror on the opposite wall. Ought to get a haircut, he thought. He never let it get this long, not in years, not since the early 70s before the Army. Must keep reminding himself to call the barber, setup an appointment — or maybe drive over and walk in. The wife didn't need the car today. She'd said so at breakfast. It was her day off. But he knew as the hours slid by he would forget to do either. He forgot to do a lot of things these days. Awareness of these memory lapses bothered him, but not so much that he sought the advice of a doctor. Timmons understood deep down there was nothing organically wrong with his brain. He'd simply lost the urge or the energy to keep things — unimportant things — in his head for long. This was the way things sorted out now, the way time fell away, escaping down the rabbit hole opening up at his feet with every step he took.

Timmons looked down at the Colt Model 1911 lying in a wooden box on the bed next to him.

What should he do with it?

He picked it up. Felt the weight. The force. The black hole gravity lock.

What did they use now? Barretta M9s.

Timmons snorted. Italian garbage that.

What should he do with it?

Put it away before the wife caught him playing with it again.

Wainwright put the weapon back in the box, closed the lid

and locked it. He stood up and noticed an erection. A giggle escaped thin lips. The old divining rod sensed a lay line. How long had it been since he last made love to the wife? So long he couldn't remember; so long he didn't bother asking her anymore. Wainwright put the box back in the closet and went over to the wife's bureau. He took out a pair of pink panties, clean new ones, and sat down again on the bed.

He stared at his reflection for some time and realized he was hungry. He glanced at the Linden. Lunch should be ready soon if the wife was on her game. He sniffed the panties more out of form than from anything else. She hadn't worn them yet of course. He masturbated in them for a long time — too long.

"Hon! Lunch is ready." The wife's footsteps on the stairs.

"Flying-fucking-Jesus!" He hadn't finished, hadn't gotten over the hump. That was getting harder to do all the time. Why?

The footsteps were rising to the door. Why hadn't he locked the damned thing?

Wainwright neared panic. He must get rid of the panties. Where? Not under the bed, she always found them there, bitched at him for it.

Put them back in the bureau. No time. She was almost at the door. He couldn't let her see them in his hand, couldn't let her see him naked. Wainwright's toenails were long and yellow and sharp. They caught in cotton fabric, tore little holes as he pulled the panties over his big feet and up over his skinny rear end.

The wife's hand was on the doorknob. No time to put his trousers on. He grabbed them off the floor and held them out in front of him.

The door opened a crack. A blue eye peeked in "What are you doing, hon?"

"Getting . . . getting dressed."

"Why?"

Because I want to, you fucking stupid cunt!

"Because it's lunch time."

The blue eye squeezed in puzzlement. "Okay . . . well hurry up."

"I'll be right down."

The eye disappeared from the door and footsteps marked each descending stair.

Wainwright breathed a sigh of relief as he put his trousers on. He forgot he was wearing the wife's panties until the next day.

The Linden Triple Chime ticked on.

"TIM, YOU HAVE to get up and do something. You can't just keep sitting here."

Wainwright rubbed sleep out of his eyes and sat up in his chair. The television program he'd been watching about the wreck of a nineteenth century steamship off the New England coast had ended. There was something else on now, a story about . . . something. He couldn't make it out exactly; the echo of the wife's voice still rang in his ears obscuring everything else. He cleared his throat and looked at her. "What?"

The wife closed her eyes for a moment, took a breath. "You've got to get up and going. You can't sit here, day after day, night after night, doing nothing. Not moving, not... not *doing*."

"Dear, what are you talking about?" Wainwright was still too sleep-bound to raise his shield of indignation. He had lost twenty pounds since leaving the Army; his cheeks were sunken hollows and his eyes maintained a glazed, damp look as if he suffered from a constant, torpid fever.

The wife sat down on the arm of the chair. "I know how depressed you are —"

"Excuse me?" Wainwright's indignation fully deployed. "I am not depressed!"

"Then why aren't you doing something? I know that Willy—"

"You don't need to bring my son into this!"

135

"*Our* son," the wife replied quietly.

"What is it — exactly— that you expect me to do? I'm retired — as you well know."

"Tim, you're too young to be retired. The Army pension isn't exactly keeping us in the lap of luxury. Without my job —"

"Your job? How many years did I have to support this family while you went to school? While you jumped from one hospital or nursing home or . . . or first aid station to another?"

"Tim, I'm a nurse." A bit of color crept into the wife's cheeks. "The Army moved us around quite a bit. I had no choice but to change jobs."

A strand of pale, too-long hair fell across Wainwright's nose. He swept it back angrily. "Yes, yes. There's always an explanation for everything, isn't there?"

"What? What does that mean?"

Wainwright's left hand jerked, knocking a glass of iced tea off the little stand next to his chair and splashing the contents on the wife's dress.

She jumped to her feet. "Tim! What in God's name!"

"An accident!" He squealed.

"You did it on purpose! What's wrong with you?"

Wainwright's eyes rolled in his head. "Not a goddamned fucking thing you *stupid, cunt-frothing-cunt*! If you didn't bring me the fucking glass of piss-tea in the first place, none of this would have happened! I didn't ask for it, you smelly bitch! I didn't ask for it!"

This shocked the wife beyond the point of speech. She backed away from him, slowly, and left the room. The Linden ceased to be wound. It gathered dust and insects and fell silent. Zinc dissolved into nothingness and the shiny brass tarnished.

THE RUNNING YEARS had a magical effect on Wainwright's skin, making it impervious to sunlight. No amount of exposure could produce any variation in a corpse-white pallor.

The frail rays of a late autumn afternoon stood no chance whatsoever, rendered doubly impotent by the tattered sheets of clouds hanging low over the few, widely dispersed homes in the village of Dawes (pronounced *Dawls* for some reason known only to the locals).

Wainwright, crouched behind a tree in his neighbor's yard, read a newspaper *borrowed* from a delivery tube in their driveway. The gray man did not wear a coat. The cold made his blue-veined hands tremble and the newspaper rattle. Sinewless limbs and a long tapering torso, which bulged in unexpected places, gave him the appearance of a praying mantis. Fifty-six-odd years of wear and tear had left a bitter impression. He looked ten years older at least. His clothes were frayed and shabby — like the man.

He fought his way to the *Help Wanted* section of the classifieds. Bloodless lips quivered as he scanned down the page, searching for something — anything — he might qualify for.

One advertisement caught his eye. It read:

Blythewood School for Exceptional Students in Wessex now hiring.

Rewarding career counseling special needs adolescents in a caring, therapeutic environment. Full time Childcare Worker positions available on all shifts. Competitive pay and benefit package. Free Meals. Call 1-866-555-2640 or apply in person at main office, Monday — Friday, 9 a.m. to 4 p.m. Experience preferred, but not required.

Wainwright gave a yelp of delight.

Free meals!

There was another ad on the next column for a position at the Kilburn School for At Risk Adolescents. It didn't mention free meals, but it might be worth a call in case the first one didn't pan out.

The newspaper, already damaged, was dealt the coup de' gras

when he ripped out the page. He stuffed the wadded remains back into the delivery tube as if this would conceal its violation. Then off for home he went, the precious scrap from the classifieds clutched in his white talon.

THAT EVENING HE stood at the kitchen sink beneath the yellow glare of a bare bulb dangling from the ceiling. A crabbed index finger moved with mechanical regularity between nostrils, conducting his thoughts.

A coat.

The first thing he needed.

He could not march into a job interview at this time of year in a short-sleeved shirt or a long-sleeved one for that matter. Appearances were important and first impressions sometimes lethal. A suit coat might work, but he'd burned his one and only after his goddamned father's goddamned funeral.

He needed a winter coat.

Wainwright stared at a lemon-yellow scab on the pad of his middle finger. Where did that come from? And where was he going to get a coat? *How* was he going to get a coat? Purchasing one was out of the question. Maybe later when he got the job, but for now... no.

Wainwright's mouth twisted into a grimace when he picked the scab and drew a tiny drop of blood.

Sometimes the ends justify the means.

The next morning Wainwright fired up his old Ford Torino and spent the rest of the day in Newbury, the county seat, on overcoat-safari. He traveled to banks, department stores, supermarkets — any place where a large number of people might gather and carelessly leave a coat untended. He received numerous second glances, and a few well-meaning citizens offered him money assuming him to be homeless. Wainwright recoiled from these charitable donations in self-righteous indignation.

"How dare you, madam! I happen to be an officer in the United States Army!"

"How dare you, sir! I am most certainly not in need of a *hot meal!*"

"Go away, little boy! I don't need your sticky pennies!"

Finally, Timmons Wainwright stumbled onto the happy hunting ground.

The Red Cross was hosting a Holiday blood drive at the Newbury Polish-American club. Wainwright wandered in and immediately recognized the opportunity at hand. His beady eyes darted from side to side. There were coats everywhere — mounds of coats, walls of coats — temporarily discarded by people temporarily fettered to plastic tubing and creaking canvas cots.

"Sir?" a young Red Cross volunteer approached him. She had a kind face and a tinsel turkey pinned to her blouse. "I'm sorry. We don't buy blood here."

Wainwright bristled at the presumption. "I beg pardon, Miss, but I am here to collect my nephew."

"Oh." The young woman blushed. "I'm terribly sorry."

"As you should be." Wainwright teetered on the verge of a full-scale tirade, but then he spotted what he was after. It was tan and long and in excellent shape and draped over the back of an unoccupied swivel chair at a small desk not ten feet away. "And there is his jacket right there!" Wainwright cried. "I shall take it to him!"

Wainwright brushed past the young woman, grabbed the overcoat, and headed for the nearest exit. He put faith in the belief a bold, swift strike would overwhelm any opposition. Unfortunately one of the garment's sleeves tangled around the arm of the chair. It held on like a frightened octopus.

In sudden terror Wainwright squeaked, *"Double chocolate shit! Double chocolate shit!"*

The hall grew silent. Blood donors propped themselves up on

elbows, Red Cross nurses paused with needle in hand, the busty blond volunteer who talked too much about her 'female problems' ceased dispensing sugar cookies and orange juice; all to gape at the spectacle of an old man wrestling an office chair for possession of an overcoat. Even the garment's owner — the young woman with the tinsel turkey — was shocked past the point of taking any action to maintain possession.

Then came a true hemorrhage of foul language from Wainwright's mouth — an alarmingly original if occasionally incomprehensible mix of the scatological, the blasphemous and the anatomically improbable. It rattled off the walls and echoed from the ceiling. A middle-aged man with a *Jesus Saves* pin on his lapel laughed obscenely.

The human Cuisinart of curses struggled towards the front entrance. He managed to get chair and coat through the exit and onto the pavement. Here the stubborn office furniture relinquished the fight and Wainwright made good his escape.

A few minutes later a Newbury cop interviewed a perplexed young Red Cross worker.

"I don't know, officer. He said something about his nephew, then — then he grabbed my coat and ran. I think he has Tourette's syndrome, if that helps?"

The cop looked at the young woman and scratched his head.

THREE DAYS LATER, the still-at-large outerwear-napper stood in the checkout line of the Super Price Shopper. A thin trickle of sweat ran down the back of his neck matched by a thin trickle of blood from the weeping gash in his knee. He ought to sue Blythewood for not taking proper care of their walkways and parking lot. Did they know what time of year it was? It might still be autumn in Virginia, some place down South, but not here in this part of New England. Leaving patches of ice for *anyone* to slip on. He could have broken his back...or his neck.

No. Not a lawsuit. An institution like Blythewood must have a battery of Springfield lawyers spoiling for such a contest; waiting to pounce on him like ravenous vampires (Timmons suffered a near supernatural dread of the entire civil and criminal judicial system). In addition, filing against Blythewood would surely cost him the job. The job was a certainty, the lawsuit a gamble.

Pay attention. The line is moving.

Wainwright shuffled forward. He had eight items in a red handbasket and wasn't sure he had enough money to pay for them. Anxiety produced a watery feeling in his guts as if bowel or bladder might let loose. He tried to calculate the exact amount of his purchase, plus applicable tax, but the damnable turbulence in his brain returned, confusing him, making an accurate reckoning impossible. How he hated this trial of patience and financial resources. How he despised the necessity of standing in this consumer's cattle-ramp hoping not to be embarrassed once again.

If (*When*) he captured a sweet position at Blythewood, this entire travail would never again be necessary. He would have a steady paycheck not some scrimy government pension and he could buy real food — perhaps even treat himself to a bottle of cold beer — and not have to chase every penny at the bottom of his pocket. Wainwright licked dry lips. He could taste the beer, the smooth yeasty richness tumbling over his tongue.

With practiced ease, Wainwright let slip the surly bonds of linearity and folded back to the interview at Blythewood.

"You all right?" The fat supervisor asked, a touch of annoyance in his harsh voice.

"Fine, fine." Wainwright dismissed the question with an imperious wave of his hand. He hadn't gotten the worst of the doorway collision with the filthy, nameless goblin and his bucket and spray bottle.

"Can we get on with the interview?" the supervisor asked impatiently.

What a rude man. "Please. Go ahead. It's what I'm here for."

"Oh. . . I seen you were in the Army for quite a bit." A fawning grin.

141

"Thank you for your service to our country."

Yes. A veteran, you lazy, ignorant, civilian slob. Back on your heels now, aren't you?

"You got it, Mr. McDonald." Wainwright replied evenly.

And what were your duties in the Army?" Absolute respect now.

"Have you ever had an assault rifle shoved in your face in a Cyprian airport, Mr. McDonald?"

"No." The supervisor cowered. "No."

"Well sir, I have — chasing AWOL GIs across every part of Europe and half of Asia Minor. I'd find them, counsel them, get them the help they needed, if I could, and get them back to their outfits."

"Uh, I see."

Wainwright leaned forward, exposed his teeth. "With all due respect, Mr. McDonald, I don't think you do. Not unless you were there in Cyprus, face-to-face with a very confused young man holding a weapon on you."

The supervisor couldn't meet his steady gaze. "Why did ya leave the Army?"

"National security."

"National security?"

"I can't talk about my reasons for leaving because of national security. I took an oath to uphold and defend the Constitution of the United States of America. I'm sure you understand, Mr. McDonald."

"Mr. Wainwright, which, uh, which of your many skills do ya think would best help our clients?"

"I think that's obvious. My years of counseling troubled young soldiers. Like I said."

The fat Scot (Irish? Whatever) was a fool.

The supervisor looked down at Wainwright's hands. Timmons' mother always told him he had the long tapering fingers of an artist.

"Play the git-tar, Mr. Wainwright?"

"What? Is there a position open in the music department? I just happened to have taught music appreciation in the public school system many years ago."

"No. I wish there was. Academics could use a man like you." The supervisor nervously cleared his throat. *"Do ya have any other interests, qualifications or abilities you feel might be good for our program?"* Must have learned this last bit by rote. Probably had it written down for him.

Wainwright gathered himself in the chair. "I understand, from reading the literature your HR office sent me, that a great many of these boys have been abused — sexually abused."

"That's right, though I can't get into too much of that. Our rules of client, uh, confidentiality are pretty strict."

"That's okay, Mr. McDonald. I understand. However, let me just say I know about that sort of thing on a personal level. Please don't ask me for details. Suffice it to say I know what these kids need. These children — these young men — need somebody who has been down there with them. I'm that man."

Awe struck, the supervisor sat for several moments in silence. Finally he stirred and said in a hushed tone, "That's about all I need to hear, Mr. Wainwright."

"When do I start, sir?"

"We'll notify you within twenty-four hours. Don't worry about that! Thanks for coming in. It was a real honor meetin' you." The supervisor gratefully shook his hand.

Lost in fermented reverie, Wainwright failed to notice the line ahead had cleared.

"Sir?" The plump woman behind the register tried to gain his attention.

Timmons Wainwright blinked and attempted to focus on the voice scratching his eardrums.

"Sir? Are you going to pay for those items?"

Obediently Wainwright placed the contents of his shopping basket on the counter. There were six cans of vegetable beef soup, a quart of 1% milk and a small bag of candy corn.

"You could have gone through the express aisle. Ten items or less," the woman reminded him as she began running things over the scanner.

"I see," Wainwright responded in a reedy voice. And then as always he had to say something absurd. "But there are no express aisles in real life, madam."

The woman frowned. She had no idea what he meant. Neither did he.

"That will be five-twenty-five," she said.

"COCKSUCKER!"

The woman's pudgy little mouth fell open.

Wainwright held a single greasy Lincoln between his fingertips.

The damned candy corn put him over budget.

He buried his chin in his chest, narrowed his eyes to slits, and rushed headlong out of the store leaving his groceries abandoned in a plastic bag at the end of the aisle.

The cold air and open space of the parking lot were a welcome tonic to the claustrophobic heat and bustle of the supermarket. He leaned against a car, breathing deeply. It had been a narrow escape.

Goddamn the Super Price Shopper's goddamned overpriced candy corn!

He found it hard to believe he *ever* enjoyed shopping with his wife on those long lost Saturday afternoons.

His wife.

Wainwright frowned and bit his lower lip at the thought of her.

All those endless domestic rituals they played out together which meant nothing. There were two backs bent over the garden in spring, two pair of hands hanging laundry on breezy summer days, two sets of sharp eyes on the lookout for the Christmas gift the boy had to have. All for nothing. He didn't even know where she lived anymore.

Wainwright stumbled towards his car. There was a Super Price Buster half a mile down the road. He would try again there.

This time he'd be more careful. Perhaps jellybeans cost less than candy corn. He liked them better anyway.

A teenage boy, hair flying across his face, passed in front of Wainwright. The boy was too tall and too thin and there was an odd hitch in his gait as if his bones were growing too fast for muscle and tendon to keep up.

Breath fled Wainwright's body.

Was that his son?

He stopped dead in his tracks and watched the boy disappear between parked cars.

Of course it could not be his son.

The old man, lips slightly parted and eyes closed, stood swaying like a dry stalk of winter grass in a harsh wind.

Of course it could not be his son.

Will had been such a sweet little boy, such a sweet disposition, such a sweet smile beneath those beautiful blue eyes and mop of blonde hair.

His sweet Will-o'-the-wisp....

Wainwright arrived ten minutes late for his job interview at Kilburn School. This wasn't much of a concern. Showing up at all qualified as a polite nod to professional etiquette. Utterly calm for once he chatted pleasantly with a nice woman named Jennifer. A sweetheart. Reminded him a little of the wife when she was young. The interview went well, not that it mattered. No free meals offered at Kilburn. A deal breaker. Jennifer assured him she would be in touch but it might take two weeks due to the time of the year (staff and student vacations) and the number of applicants. The day after Thanksgiving at the latest she promised. She thanked him for his interest and wished him a happy holiday. He knew it was a courteous brush off and didn't care.

Wainwright returned home an hour later — in time to pick up the bedroom telephone on the last ring.

The caller introduced herself as Arlene O'Connor from

Blythewood School.

A bag of licorice jellybeans spilled on the dirty floor. A few moments later they were stomped into a sugary black paste — a feast for mice — in a wild rage-fueled jig.

BRIGHT MORNING LIGHT filtering through the louvered vents and grimy windows of the attic found Wainwright genuflecting on a boney knee before an ancient wooden trunk. He lifted the heavy banded lid and stared for a moment at the contents: pictures drawn by a child's hand, loose photographs and neat photo albums, worn baseball cards and small toys, precious once, round aluminum cans of 8mm home movies, a wedding dress beneath, and other things, too many....

He lifted a photo of the wife and son.

He recognized the woman and didn't. She was a pretty stranger and it hurt his head to place this fading image somewhere in his faded memory. There was a needle sharp image of champagne in a crystal glass catching fire from a flaring candle. The wedding? Maybe an anniversary. Timmons had to let it go. But the little boy he knew. He felt again the day, the hour, the moment he had taken the photo of him, remembered the sound of the boy's voice, more than an echo, fresh in his ear, saw the boy dancing from foot to foot, boundless life and energy mocking any attempt to capture them in a picture.

Piece by piece, without self-conscious prompting, he emptied the trunk, neatly setting everything adrift on a sea of cracked pine board. For some time he watched these objects with a keen eye, waiting for them to resurrect the past, spin the substance of existence out of dust and mold and bat droppings. Not a flicker teased his eye. Finally, he began putting things back where they belonged, hidden from sight. His fingers moved slowly at first then frantically, like broken twigs kicked by the wind. When the task was done, boney arms formed a square over the top of the trunk. Wainwright's head drooped and he slept for a brief time on his knees — until the hot asphalt of dreams scalded him awake.

Later in the day the old brown Torino rattled to a stop beside pump number 2 at the Dawes Cumberland Farms. The engine coughed and eventually fell silent. The driver side door swung open on rusted hinges. Wainwright climbed out, stiffly, like a quadriplegic whose limbs are stimulated to movement by powerful electrodes. It was two days since the phone call from Blythewood. No, not a phone call. A dagger to the heart. He mumbled to himself as he thumbed through a few ratty dollars on his way inside the store. He mumbled still on his way back to the car.

The gas nozzle was almost too heavy for him to manage. He struggled to seat it in the filler pipe behind the Ford's rear license plate. Pulling the trigger and holding it proved to be an equally grueling task. He braced himself against the trunk with his free hand while a tingling numbness spread up through the clenched fingers of the other and reached his shoulder. Somehow he managed to replace the hose on the pump when he finished. A long rasping breath flattened lips and nostrils. The return trip around the Torino was like circumnavigating the earth in a rowboat.

Wainwright slumped behind the wheel and wondered if he retained the strength to turn the key in the ignition. His eyes closed and he drifted.

A loud rumbling from the opposite side of the pump brought him back. A green GTO pulled in for gas. Wainwright smiled a little. 70 or 71. He'd bet on it. He'd always wanted one of those. Nice car in great condition.

The driver got out. Wainwright's face turned alarming shades of scarlet and black.

It was the Blythewood supervisor, Mr. McDonald.

Wasn't it enough for the man to deny him a livelihood? What compelled the swag-bellied Scottish pig to taunt him in public?

Anger lent strength to wind and limb. When the supervisor entered the Cumberland Farms, Wainwright snaked out of his car and slithered between the pumps. He wasn't sure what he intended to do, but he must do something.

Pee on the car door handle? No, he didn't have to make.

Smash the glass? That would take a hammer — Merciful Heavens, there was a Cornwall landfill sticker on the windshield. The brute was practically a neighbor. Cornwall was no more than ten miles down the road from Dawes.

Scratch up the pretty paint? Oh, wouldn't Old McDonald have a cow. Wainwright slapped at his pants pockets for his keys. He'd left them in the Torino. No time to get them now. He took a deep breath and clawed furiously at the GTO's hood and fender with jagged fingernails. This didn't do much but it was a gesture at least.

Wainwright scrambled back into his car and waited. He watched McDonald exit the store, watched him fuel up, watched him not notice the invisible scratches, watched him drive away.

"Rotten bastard," Timmons whispered and started the Ford. He had half a mind to follow McDonald but realized he'd never catch him. The Torino was no match for the Pontiac and the swine undoubtedly drove like a maniac, heedless of other motorists' safety.

On his way back home, Wainwright imagined *Mr. McDonald's* laughter as he gleefully related the details of his sick little prank to all his grinning cronies back at Blythewood.

"Yeah, told the old fuck he had the job, and then dropped the old yellow hammer on him!"

It was too much. Wainwright forced a clenched fist into his mouth, fighting an urge to vomit. No man should be asked to bear this kind of cruelty. What was wrong with a world in which creatures like *Mr. McDonald* wallowed in their own stew, unrepentant and unpunished?

Whores and booze and dirty penises — the currency of such men. And yet... and yet they dared lay claim to superiority over others, flaunted their power to give and take the bread out of another's mouth — out of *his* mouth.

Wainwright cursed the reeking wombs of the mothers who gave birth to such dirty, filthy scum, to such—

"FUCKING-CUM-GLUTTON-SONS-OF-BITCHES!"

Overcome by the force of his emotios, Timmons Wainwright swooned and bruised his forehead on the hard rubber ridges of the Torino's big steering wheel.

The rusty Ford wandered off the road. It dropped two wheels in a ditch and came to rest.

Daddy?

"I'm right here, boy!"

It's too dark to see, Daddy.

"No, it isn't! I'm right here!"

I can't find you.

"Yes you can, son! Keep trying!"

Daddy? I can't see you. It's too dark, Daddy... it's too dark... too dark....

Timmons Wainwright bolted upright in bed, hands outstretched in a desperate effort to grasp the reedy voice ebbing away in the blackness. He tried to follow and fell out of bed. Like scrambled eggs in a frying pan he lay on the floor until morning.

TIMMONS PULLED BACK the curtain ever so slightly and peered through the dirty window. He watched the new postman make his delivery. Wainwright did not like the set of the man's ears; they hung too low and had tufts of hair on them. It gave the fellow a suspiciously simian appearance. When the carrier got back in his tricked-out golf cart and drove away Wainwright slipped cautiously out to the dilapidated porch. A skinny, half-grown

149

yellow cat scurried over to him, meowing in a strained voice. This was not a pet but rather a stray that wandered onto the property and refused to leave. Wainwright gave it a few scraps and a bit of milk when he could spare them. This was not such a bountiful day.

The old man bent down and scratched the top of the cat's head. "Sorry, puss-puss. Nothing for you this morning." Wainwright straightened and retrieved two envelopes from the lopsided mailbox hanging by a single finishing nail next to the door. He clutched the letters against his chest not daring to look at them yet and slid back into the house.

There were a few deep breaths and a faint tremor running from the top of Wainwright's shoulders all the way down to his hands before he finally summoned the courage to examine the envelopes. One correspondence was from New England Electric demanding back payments. This did not disturb him. He knew the company could not shut off his power during the winter months. He tossed the notice into a shabby wicker wastebasket on the floor.

The other envelope, however, caused him swift and near overwhelming anxiety. It was from NorCentral Mortgage and it demanded $4,465.34 in back mortgage payments within the next sixty days or his home, the only thing he owned in the world (other than the old Torino), would be foreclosed upon.

Timmons Wainwright grew dizzy. He staggered towards the living room and the only *seat* in the house, a dusty Soloflex his wife bought him years ago. He used it twice for its intended purpose; exercise proved too strenuous and painful. After those early days of good intentions, it became merely static furniture, the only solid piece in the room. Wainwright fell on it like an unstrung marionette. The letter from NorCentral fluttered to his feet. The old man held his head in his hands and softly wept.

What was he to do? What *could* he do?

He believed forcible eviction, like termination of utilities, was prohibited during the winter, but it was only a stay of execution. Come spring he would be homeless. No job, no house — nothing. If only he'd gotten the position at Blythewood then he might have been able to hold off the mortgage company, make automatic payroll deductions . . . something.

Wainwright liked to think all people deep down were decent if you gave them half a chance. But damned Mr. McDonald? He was the devil himself.

Wainwright swallowed his sobs and wiped his nose on the sleeve of his shirt. Why was it so hard to figure things out these days, make it all run properly? Back in the Army he enjoyed status, confidence, the ability to get the job done, no matter how difficult it might be.

But now… but now….

The dizziness relented and he climbed to his feet. Wearily he trudged from one room to the next, past a few wobbly card tables cluttered with old books and odds and ends, past stacked bags of garbage he hadn't snuck into neighbors' garbage cans yet. The walls were empty of everything but grime — no pictures, no paintings, no photographs. They'd been taken down and burned out back along with the furniture the wife didn't take when she left. The floors were stained and gritty as if a thin layer of sand had been scattered over everything. He eventually arrived at the bathroom. He stared at the rust stained toilet for a long moment and then removed the cracked lid from the water tank. Inside, tightly sealed in a plastic bag wrapped with duct tape, was a bundle of twenties, fifties, and hundreds. Wainwright stuck his hand in the cold water and removed the package.

How much? he wondered. Forty-nine-hundred? Or five thousand even?

The old man shook his head sadly. Not quite enough to buy the bit of marble for his son. Oh, he could purchase a less costly monument to be sure, but his son deserved the best a father could afford to give him — in death if not life. It had taken Timmons Wainwright years of scrimping and scraping to reach the point where a decent memorial was within reach.

Wainwright put the money back in the water tank. Forty-nine-hundred or five thousand, it didn't matter. The money wasn't his to spend. It belonged to the dead.

Finance one hell of a drinking jag though.

Where did that come from? What in the name of all things holy was he thinking about? Booze away his son's money?

Wainwright replaced the lid and wobbled back to the living room. An old tape player sat on the floor next to the Soloflex. He sagged onto the bench and reached down to press the play button. The tinny ghost of Sinatra began singing through crackling distortion. Sometimes the music soothed Wainwright, but not today, not under these circumstances. He rocked back and forth for a few moments, eyes half open. The tremors in his arms and neck and hands increased. He shut off the tape player and picked up the notice from the mortgage company, to read it one more time, to find some overlooked loophole, some tiny spark of hope. The consummate futility of this act slowly registered in his mind. Like a teakettle on high boil, a stream of foul language began hissing from his lips.

The cold, corporate knife-in-the-jugular was maniacally torn to pieces and tossed on the floor. A tornado-shrieking Wainwright then dropped his pants, grappled with his crabbed member and pissed on the shredded remains. An impromptu victory-dance around the soggy pile of confetti followed.

In the frenzy Wainwright neglected to pull up his trousers which quickly became tangled around his feet.

He fell face first into the befouled notice of foreclosure.

Now he'd been served — and had his nose rubbed in it.

The next day Wainwright had the good fortune to run afoul

of two lesbians and their shared boyfriend. It was well past noon. Timmons stood in front of his house staring off into nothing. The skinny cat twined around his ankles. It eventually gave up for lack of response and wandered off. A cold breeze plucked at his sleeve and reddened his hands and face to no effect. Blank, watery eyes did not register the Chrysler LeBaron when it pulled up in front of him.

Gradually, he became aware of someone calling his name. He licked seared lips and started for his front door.

"Mr. Wainwright! Wait a minute!" A blonde girl, maybe nineteen or twenty, popped out of the LeBaron and rushed towards him. Brief terror made Timmons cringe, but he turned and held his ground.

"Mr. Wainwright, it's me. Cat Johnston."

He vaguely recognized her. She was from Dawes. One of the natives' daughter. But Cat? Cat wasn't a name. It was an animal. A pet. A stray. No one named his or her child Cat.

"Listen, I've got a favor to ask you, Mr. Wainwright." Her eyes flickered a momentary brightness which masked their naturally dull aspect.

"What?" he croaked. *Go away, girl.*

"A favor. I was wondering if you'd do something for me." A giggle quivered on her too-large mouth. "We'll be happy to pay you." She gestured at the young woman and young man sitting in the LeBaron. They were engaged in trying to conceal laughter.

Was this a trap? "Pay me? How much?"

"Yeah, like twenty-five dollars."

Twenty-five dollars would buy gas. Gas to get him back and forth to Cornwall.

"Do you want to buy something from me?" The white noise in his head made it hard to pay attention.

"Just your time. We want you to come back to our house and watch me and Dasha get it on while Jimmy takes pitchers." She evidenced no hesitation or embarrassment in making this request. Were she capable of such an emotion, it certainly wouldn't be wasted on a nobody, a zero, a cracked old geezer like Wainwright.

"Get it on?"

"Yeah, you know, *do it*. You pretend to be my dad comin' home and catchin' me getting' messy with Dasha. We're gonna send the pitchers to some magazines in California. They pay big bucks for that kind of thing. Lezzy stuff especial. Shit the pitchers might go up on the web. Real money there, too."

"*Pictures*. The web?" Wainwright floated high over Never Never Land. Her next words kicked him all the way to Pluto.

"You can spank me, if you want to. I don't mind. The mags like the whole incest angle too. You know, daddy's naughty little girl and what not. We'll give you an extra ten and a bottle of schnapps if you do." A glossy black nail with a little fake diamond glued to it pointed at him. "But you gotta change into something else. That coat. Man, you in drag or what? Put somethin' on that makes you look like you *could* be my dad. Got anything nice?"

"Nice?"

"Yeah, like a suit or something that makes you look . . . well, you know."

He didn't. His mouth hung open. Possibly he didn't comprehend what she said, possibly 'twenty-five dollars' were the only words spinning around in the Scarecrow's hat.

She took this dumbfounded expression to indicate eager acquiescence.

"Go put it on and let's get goin'," she commanded. "I'm hot and ready."

Mystified, and apparently bereft of free will, he turned and went into his house, returning a few minutes later wearing his dress blues, dove grey gloves and a pair of dirty, once-white cross trainers. It was the best he could muster. The garments were in immaculate condition but no longer fit his withered frame. He looked like the remains of the Unknown Soldier risen from the tomb and given a fresh uniform.

"Daddy's back from the war!" the girl squealed in delight. "Daddy's back from the war!"

The next thing Wainwright knew, he stood at parade rest in a smelly, disheveled bedroom. Behind his back, a straining fist clutched two tens and a five. He tried not to watch the girls slobber and groan and poke at each other but it proved impossible. The odor of sex curled in his nostrils and a bulge grew in his trousers. Jimmy's expensive camera flashed with relentless monotony.

The old soldier held his position until Jimmy dropped the camera and his pants and jumped into bed with the girls. It was then Wainwright beat the retreat before he took a direct hit from flying fluids.

The daylight was already beginning to fail as Wainwright hurried down the road to his home. Frigid dust kicked at his heels. Tears stained his stubbled cheeks. He wanted to run but only managed a lame trot. By the time he reached his door, he blubbered and gasped like a small child. The wad of cash fell from his nerveless hand. He left it there on the porch and went inside. After gagging over the sink, he carefully put the uniform in a garment bag and hung it in the closet. Then he sat on the bed, wept a little more and furiously — shamefully — masturbated.

Before sleep claimed him that night, he went out to the porch with a cracked, flickering flashlight and found the ball of money behind the leg of a rotted Adirondack chair. The dreary autumn wind hadn't stolen it away as he feared, merely hidden it.

Twenty-five dollars would buy the gas he needed.

ON SATURDAY, ONE day after the first big snow of the season, Timmons Wainwright parked his Torino down the street from MacDonnell's house. It took little effort to track the

Blythewood supervisor to his lair. Wainwright stopped at the Cornwall Stewarts Bread and Butter Shoppe and asked at the counter.

"McDonald or MacDonnell?" the teenage pimple with a buzz cut asked as he rang up Wainwright's pack of gum.

Not sure how to respond, Timmons nodded.

"Well, Mike MacDonnell lives up on Main Street. Can't miss it. Big white house with pillars. If he's home, that Goat of his will be in the driveway." The kid's eyes narrowed a little. "You say you're a friend of his?" The villagers maintained a natural suspicion of outsiders asking about people.

"Of course. Mr. *MacDonnell* and I have been friends for many years." Why couldn't the fat Blythewood supervisor stick to one pronunciation? Trying to hide something?

"He's your friend and you call him mister?"

"Old habit." Wainwright managed a smile of sorts. "We were in the Navy together. He was my commanding officer."

"He's a lot younger than you, and I don't recall ever hearing about him being in the Navy," the kid remarked skeptically.

"I said I was his commanding officer." Timmons responded slyly, silently congratulating himself on turning the tables on the ignorant counter jockey.

The kid shook his head and handed Wainwright the gum.

Now, like a patient hunter, Wainwright sat in the dwindling afternoon light, watching for his prey to stir. This was the second day of surveillance. The Nor'easter curtailed Wainwright's efforts on the previous morning. A small notepad rested next to him on the bench seat, filled with rambling observations on MacDonnell's habits and behavior. Most of it was little more than wild speculation. There were also a few stained envelopes grabbed from a garbage pail. He'd examined these utility bills with a careful and critical eye. Timmons believed it gave him great insight into his prey's psychology. How it did so posed a question Wainwright neither asked himself nor answered.

Directly across from Wainwright's position, on the porch of a rundown yellow house, a redheaded girl, about sixteen, paced restlessly, waiting for a date to arrive. The girl wore an unzipped down-jacket from which plump breasts protruded like a clutch of helium balloons. The girl was cute but not destined for any kind of lasting beauty. Bad nutrition and numerous pregnancies — the enduring curses of poor rural communities — would quickly steal the brief glow of physical attractiveness she now enjoyed.

Wainwright glanced in her direction a few times, drawn more by the flicker of movement in his peripheral vision than by any interest in her feminine attributes. There were more important things on his mind. The ex-Army officer had finally settled on a course of action and dubbed it 'Operation Spoilsport.'

During his years in the military, Timmons Wainwright had come into contact with a few Air Force nuke-techs, those gruesome little men who liked to read science fiction novels when they were not cheerfully maintaining the instruments of a real-life Armageddon. Wainwright despised their mindless zeal and loathsome self-importance, but this distaste did not prevent him from listening to their tales. One story they told, however dubious the authenticity might be, concerned a secret government program called *Spoilsport*. Six months — some of the techs said a year — after the total nuclear annihilation of the United States in a devastating first strike by a hostile power, an elegantly simple and self-reliant computer would activate hidden missile silos in the Midwest and launch an automated counter strike against all enemy targets around the world.

Spoilsport — nobody wins if America loses.

Operation Spoilsport — nobody wins if Timmons Wainwright loses. And Timmons Wainwright was dead tired of losing.

The old man thought he detected movement in the window of MacDonnell's house and quickly raised his opera glasses. These ancient magnifiers were of little use, no more than a family heirloom handed down from his mother. A pair of decent binoculars would have been preferred, but too costly.

There was no activity in MacDonnell's window. A trick of the light, nothing more. Wainwright lowered the opera glasses with a silent curse born on a sigh.

An explosive hammering on the roof of the Ford rocked the vehicle with the force of a small earthquake. Wainwright dropped the glasses on the floor.

A hairy Neanderthal brandishing a hockey stick stood at the Torino's rear bumper. The man lacked coat and shoes and he was exceedingly angry about something. His primal screams of rage vibrated the car's sealed windows.

"What are you — some sort a' frickin' peevert?" The hairy man brought the hockey stick crashing down on the roof again.

Wainwright's hands shook as he fumbled for the keys in the ignition.

"Starin' at my daughter's tits, you frickin' homo? I'm gonna bust your damned head!" The apelike figure swung again. The Torino's rear, driver side window shattered.

Timmons squealed and tried to start the car. It moaned and sputtered.

And then there was another man — black eyes, high cheek bones (*a miniature Apache?*) — off to his right chucking snowballs at the windshield, yelling something about *dirty socks.*

"Frickin' faggot!" The hairy man's last slap shot was so vigorous he lost his footing in the snow and fell heavily, smashing his forehead against the side of the Ford. He slumped to the ground, bleeding and dazed.

The miniature Apache ran to his aid and from the porch the redheaded girl cried out something.

The Torino's still game 351 Windsor finally turned over and Wainwright hit the gas. His breathing didn't return to normal until he crossed the border into Massachusetts. He changed his pants the moment he got home.

LESSON LEARNED. IT was two days before Wainwright recovered the nerve to return to Cornwall. Procedural changes were implemented. He came after dark and parked three houses up from his previous observation post out of fearful respect for the hairy, stick wielding troll and his Apache sidekick. The plastic sheet clumsily duct-taped over the rear window was an eloquent and sometimes drafty reminder of that harrowing incident. Given the Torino's position and the encompassing darkness, little relieved by a few widely dispersed street lamps, Wainwright wasn't able to observe much of anything. It didn't matter. It was the effort that counted, the willingness to carry on.

Timmons Wainwright held up a plastic lighter and peered myopically at two mimeographed sheets of paper in his hands:

US Army Special Forces
Standing Orders of Rodgers' Rangers
(Major Robert Rodgers, 1759)
   1. Don't forget nothing
   2. Have your musket clean as a whistle, hatchet scoured, sixty rounds powder and ball, and be ready to march at a minute's warning.
   3. When you're on the march, act the way you would if you was sneaking up on a deer. See the enemy first.
   4. Tell the truth about what you see....

Wainwright rubbed his bulbous forehead. Such bad grammar in such a top-notch commander. He carefully folded the sheets and tucked them in the pocket of his coat next to the Colt.

It was nearly time to implement Operation Spoilsport. A few days and then....

Then....

Wainwright admitted he was getting too old to be out every night on a mission; the winter cold was starting to eat away at his bones and turn his skin into freeze-dried cauliflower. But soon enough none of it would matter. The time of reckoning was at hand. Plans were coming together, and by taking shape, suggesting the possible consequences to the enemy and the enemy's subsequent reactions.

One thing did bother him this night. On the way to Cornwall he noticed a great many houses decked out in Christmas lights and decorations, even a fully festooned tree or two (likely artificial he assumed, a fire hazard if not) twinkling in the odd window. Couldn't people let the holidays proceed naturally? Was it necessary to graft Christmas onto Thanksgiving? When he was a boy there was an order to things, a stately processional of seasonal celebrations which allowed one to savor each unique moment, form clear, clean memories.

Timmons wiggled his chilly toes and wondered if he should have found another pair of socks to wear.

What would Major Rodgers think? Likely compliment Wainwright on his ingenuity and willingness to persevere in spite of near unbearable physical discomfort.

Old Robert Rodgers... what a man... what a great leader of men... what a true hero. Too bad he died a drunk. The Irish and their booze....

Wainwright's chin drifted down to his chest and he abruptly fell asleep.

It wasn't a bitter night in Cornwall and he wore the coat *donated* by the Red Cross. This combination allowed him to escape hypothermia.

A BUZZING ANXIETY grew in Wainwright as

Thanksgiving drew near, reached a zenith of cognitive dissonance the Wednesday night before his personal D-Day. Sleep proved impossible. Anticipation and organic confusion turned his brain into a bowling alley of conflicting thoughts and emotions. He rolled from one side of the bed to the other, compulsively picked his nose until it bled and then picked it some more; kicked his feet out from beneath the blanket only to dig them under again when they grew cold a few moments later. It was a purgatory of sorts, but no prayers issued forth from the faithful for the release of his soul.

Most maddeningly a fragment of a poem kept running through his brain He remembered neither the author nor any but the last two lines:

That I may make one angry sound
Before I vanish into silence

Finally, he found a measure of comfort and cerebral organization in telling himself the story of how tomorrow would resolve. Everything would go according to plan; no glitches, no hitches and the ending would write itself. This story quickly became something else: an alternative reality every bit as genuine, every bit as solid and authentic as the confines of his house, more so. He could see the colors of this other world, smell the air and hear the sounds — interact….

MacDonnell spots a car, hazard lights flashing, pulled over in the breakdown lane. A split second of indecision — whether to pass by or stop and help — rendered moot by a tall, graceful figure stepping out from behind the disabled vehicle.

MacDonnell slows to a halt alongside the other car. To his surprise, he recognizes the figure: the distinguished gentleman from the job interview. What is his name? A sick feeling settles in MacDonnell's stomach. He is ashamed, but smothers it in arrogant self-denial.

"Do you need some help?" he asks. Vaunting arrogance now. He doesn't care if he is identified.

161

"My car's broken down."

A ghastly smile paints itself on MacDonnell's face. It makes him look like a stroke victim waiting for a dietary-aide to bring a bowl of lemon sherbet. "I think we've met — at Blythewood?"

"Yes. We've met. At Blythewood."

The tone, or lack of it, in the tall, graceful man's voice makes MacDonnell a trifle uncomfortable on several conscious and subconscious levels. He's never been good at remembering names. He's not bright, but feels compelled to try. "Timothy Wainwright?"

"Timmons Wainwright!" There is thunder in that proud name.

MacDonnell's head jerks away from the open window in an involuntary reaction to this righteous flash of indignity. "Right, Timmons. Well, it's, uh, nice to see you again. Can I give you a lift somewhere — to a telephone or a service station?"

"Yes. That would be... kind of you." The trap begins to close.

"Hop in. D&K Auto is just down the road a few miles. They might still be open."

The Pontiac smells as expected: semen and booze and sweaty, feverish ego.

"What's wrong with your car?" MacDonnell tries to make small talk as they get underway. Not good at it, too self-involved and inherently stupid.

"How do I know, Mr. MacDonnell? I wasn't a motor pool officer."

They drive the rest of the way in silence. MacDonnell offers his passenger a beer which is refused with a stony, silent dignity.

D&K Auto turns out to have a lot full of cars awaiting repair and not a light on in the building.

"Oh, gosh. I don't know what to tell you," MacDonnell mumbles. Then reluctantly, "Guess I could give you a ride home — if you don't live too far."

"Unexpectedly generous of you, Mr. MacDonnell. Unexpected."

"We better be on our way."

"Of course we should."

A few minutes later they arrive in Dawes. The car stops in front of the house. "Here you go."

"Get out of the vehicle, hands up, Mr. MacDonnell."

"Scuse me?"

"There's no excuse for you!"

The Model 1911 Automatic appears and commands the moment.

"What the heck are you doing?" MacDonnell bawls, barely containing an urge to cover his face with both arms. The muzzle of the big ACP does not waver.

"Get out of the car as instructed."

MacDonnell obeys. He's wearing a too-tight sports sweatshirt. Damnable New York Yankees of course. It doesn't cover the soft rolls of his belly. There is a urine stain spreading down from his zipper. All the plotting and stalking, all the frustrations and painful accidents along the way, have finally born fruit. The capture of Nemesis, of Moriarty, of Brutus — of Judas is achieved.

"Jesus Christ! Put that thing down!" MacDonnell is about to further befoul his pants. He is entirely convinced this is no joke, no hoax. There is steel in the eyes behind the Colt.

"No, you filthy whoremaster. You don't give orders here. This is my office, not yours."

Now MacDonnell knows. There will be no sorting things out. He is the mouse caught in the falcon's claws.

"Look, Mr. Wainwright," MacDonnell says in a shaky voice. "I'm not sure what's going on here, but if it's about the job, I have been reconsidering."

"You're pathetic. Abandon any idea about making a run for it. Be advised, Mr. MacDonnell, I am quite adept in the use of sidearms. Don't forget, while you were spending your formative years jerking-off in dirty socks to Wonder Woman comic books, I was serving in the armed forces of this great nation. Weapons are no mystery to me."

"Look, Timothy—"

"Timmons, you brainless flubberbag."

"Sorry!"

"Timmons was my mother's maiden name. They were a very fine, very respectable family from Maine — landed there in 1692. My dear mother did not give me that good name for you to make a mockery of it."

"Said I was sorry." MacDonnell will physically grovel in the driveway if it is demanded.

"Not so high and mighty now, are we, Mr. MacDonnell? Spell it for me — T-I-M-M-O-N-S!"

The Blythewood supervisor does as he is commanded.

"Very good. Now, up on the porch." A casual wave of the automatic's muzzle is all the motivation needed. "Hands on top of your head, please."

On the top step, MacDonnell turns around, slowly, and whines, "Why are you doing this?"

"Why? I suppose even you deserve an explanation. I've been following you for days, Mr. MacDonnell. I know where you live, what hours you work, where you buy your hooch — and all about the poor, deluded little leg-spreader you forced into marriage. She would thank me for this were she ever to know. Perhaps I shall send her an anonymous letter one day. We shall see. But let me continue. It is no accident my car broke down at that particular location. I was prepared to wait there, for as many nights as necessary, until you fell into my trap. I had no idea you would accommodate me on the first try. However, there you were, a slave to habit and lustful appetites.

"I've known men like you my whole life, Mr. MacDonnell — envious, greedy, always trying to climb up the ladder of success on someone else's back. Ooooh, yes! I've taken your measure, my friend. I know your ilk. And you knew what I could do for the boys at Blythewood, didn't you? Lap dogs like you can smell capability in others. It is what makes you so dangerous. You had to stop me to preserve yourself. What lies did you weave for your superiors, what dark perjuries? You're a master of deception and a king of fraud, Mr. MacDonnell."

"And you're ass-over-teakettle nuts," MacDonnell sobs.

"Yes, of course. I'm the crazy one. I've heard that calumny before. Close your hog snout and get up on the porch."

"What are you planning to do?" Snot and tears fill MacDonnell's mouth. "You gonna hurt me? You don't have to! I'll do anything you want." His meaning is clear.

"You'd like to portray me as a closet gay, driven by some violent form of

homosexual panic, wouldn't you? Give you another label to apply and dismiss me by. Sorry to disappoint you, but I was married to a fine lady. Unfortunately, she didn't have the faith to see things through to the end. But I need not justify myself further. You are just a shit-miner, seeking sad little secrets to use against others. How many troubled young soldiers have I counseled who were destroyed by rotten officers, officious bastards like you? How many fine kids did I see destroy their lives with alcohol and drugs because of vile Morlocks disguised as men. Like you. Like you."

MacDonnell pleads, *"You can have the job. You're the best I interviewed!"*

"I know I am."

MacDonnell whimpers and loses his balance. He falls on his rear end, splitting the crotch of his pants wide open. He raises his hands in supplication. *"Please. Please, God. This can't be happening…"*

"I almost feel sorry for you."

Finally a dim light is flickering in MacDonnell's inadequate mind. He grasps that life is not what he thought.

It is…. Ugly slapstick, a vicious pratfall. Like walking out your front door and getting your head broken by a falling satellite dish which brought Bugs Bunny and the World Series into your living room. Like walking through the elevator door and falling all the way to the bottom of the shaft while you scream your lungs out for help from someone who isn't there. Like a healthy, beautiful boy dying of leukemia at seventeen. Dying in agony. All of man's — every man's — secret fears are verified. Life is nothing more than a madcap scramble to stay alive: aimless, ridiculous, a matter of pretense and false significance tallied up by blind luck and random chance.

Now Mr. MacDonnell understands. Now he can die bewildered as everyone must.

From nowhere and everywhere, Sinatra starts singing:

"Start spreadin' the news —"

A voice as big and dramatic as a military brass band declared, **"That won't work, you ass! Shoot him at his door. Shoot him in the face! Shoot his whore too!"**

Momentarily startled into full wakefulness, Wainwright gradually relaxed into a restful sleep.

"Yes, shoot him at the door. And his whore too, if I must," he whispered to the whispering dark before closing his eyes.

THE FRONT DOOR of the tumble down house opened; a brief flare of yellow illumination against the encompassing murk. Wainwright stepped out and quietly closed it. A humid residue of sweat remained on the rusty knob where his hand had gripped it. He walked across the creaking porch and down the skewing steps. He stopped at the bottom in a puddle of slush and took a long breath. A single drop of rain, falling invisible from the turgid sky, landed unnoticed on the tip of his raptor nose.

Timmons took a ski mask from a coat pocket and pulled it over his head. He gagged. The wool smelled of mothballs and cinnamon and the wife's perfume. After all these years it still held her favorite scent. Remarkable. Then again she always used too much cologne.

He tapped the heavy object in the other coat pocket.

Ready.

Thanksgiving night. The end of all things. Mr. MacDonnell would be at home now, stuffing his soggy mouth with white turkey and cranberry strewn dressing and creamy potatoes, slathered all in rich gravy. But no Dutch apple pie for his dessert this night. Nor allspice-laden pumpkin smothered in whip cream.

Tonight Mr. MacDonnell would get a steel core pie in the face.

Compulsively Wainwright pulled the .45 out to check it one last time. Must make sure the magazine was seated properly and the safety off. He half-cocked the automatic, against all training and common sense, and held it up against the glow of a distant street light. All was as it should be.

But was it? Something huge and fearful moved around him in

the night. He could feel it on his skin, rippling past in a wave of static electricity.

As if to prove this apprehension, the skinny cat slipped silently from a lake of shadow and mounted Wainwright's foot and ankle. Needle claws pierced thin fabric and the skin beneath. The unexpected sensations of touch and movement reaped a strangled shriek from the old man's lips. He kicked the cat straight up in the air, and uncorked the .45 at point blank range.

The cat turned inside out. The tiny, tattered corpse flopped to the ground a few feet away.

The detonation rang in Wainwright's ears, leaving him shattered and witless. He wobbled back and forth, close to falling over. Eventually this passed and his thoughts and hearing returned. Fearfully he moved forward, scuffling at the soggy leaves with his foot until he found the cat. The old man's boney shoulders sagged and his wet eyes closed for a moment. Bloodless lips muttered something unintelligible.

The .45 felt like a ship's anchor in his hand. He put it back in the coat pocket and shuffled towards his car. He would bury the cat upon return. Or wrap it in newspaper and drop it in the Howards' trash can.

It occurred to him that someone might have heard the shot and called the State Police. That would be the last thing he needed tonight. But, no. No worry there. This evening the good folk of Dawes were all behind closed doors and windows, feasting. Unlikely anyone heard anything or paid much attention if they did. Besides, the Butler tribe over on Furnace Road touched off fireworks on every holiday, summer and winter. Wainwright was mildly surprised they hadn't lit up the sky yet. Probably too drunk to remember. The Butlers were congenital drunks.

Wainwright made five miles on the road to Cornwall before the Torino sputtered and died. The twenty-five dollars worth of gas had run out. He managed to wrestle the vehicle into the breakdown lane. For some time he sat cursing and pounding on the dashboard and periodically turning the key in the ignition. The fuel gauge still registered a quarter tank. He'd known for years the gauge wasn't to be trusted; but he'd convinced himself that tonight, of all nights, the fates would be with him.

He activated the flashers (at least they still worked) and got out of the car. The scattering drizzle grew steadier now. It didn't bother him; it seemed appropriate with everything turning to shit.

Or was it?

Wainwright took a few steps onto the highway and looked at the Torino. There it sat on the shoulder of the road, hazard lights blinking. As it had in the more-than-dream from last night.

Chills stroked his crooked spine. It was coming true. No dream. A vision. The next car over the hill would carry Mr. MacDonnell on to his fate.

He briefly wondered what could bring MacDonnell out on Thanksgiving night. Likely booze, perhaps cigarettes or condoms, if a swine like him bothered to use French Safes.

Headlights appeared from the direction of Cornwall. In deadly calm Wainwright waited until they were near, then vigorously waved his arms.

It would be the GTO....

But it wasn't. It was a Dodge half-ton driven by a man named Bud. Bud was the kind of person who always tucked his shirt in, almost always voted Republican, never missed deer season, and never passed a fellow human being stranded by the side of the road, even one wearing a ski mask.

"Hello. Can I help you there, Chief?"

"Out of gas . . . ." Wainwright forced the words. He felt phantom hands closing around his throat.

"Cripes. Heck of a night to have that happen. I can take you down to Cumbies. Got a gas can?"

"No." The word was little more than a whisper, close to a cry of despair.

"Oh. Well, let's see. You live far from here?"

"Dawes."

"Oh, cripes. That's just a hop, skip and a jump. Climb in, Chief. I'll get you home. Better turn off them flashers. You don't want to wear down the battery. Car's off the road far enough. Nobody gonna run into it."

"Thank you." Wainwright replied mechanically. A moment later, weightless, and nearly blind, he climbed into the cab.

"I got heat if you're cold, Chief." Bud pointed at Wainwright's head.

"Oh, yes…." Wainwright removed the ski mask and stuffed it in a pocket. There was a growing pain in his chest. "I'm not cold."

Bud put the Dodge on the road. "You from around here?"

"I was born in Newbury."

"Yeah? Me too. Live in Chatham now. Whaddya do for a livin'?"

"Retired from the Army."

"Yeah? I'm a welder myself these days. Worked out there at the Ford plant on Green Island after I did my stint in the Corps. Worked at the Watervliet Arsenal for a good long time too. Helped make the big guns for them battle wagons. Only place on earth still makes 'um."

Please, please shut up. "Thank you again, sir. This is very kind."

"Oh, cripes. No problem. Man should be with his family on Thanksgiving. I'm on my way home now. Comin' back from Hoosick Falls. My mother's in a nursing home there. Nice place. Small. She's ninety-two. Would you believe it? Got the Alzheimer's, though. She don't recognize me these days. Don't really talk. We couldn't keep her home no more." Bud grew quiet for a moment. "Man should be with his family."

Wainwright nodded agreement. "I should be with my son." The chest pains peaked and subsided.

"Got kids, huh? Me too. Three of 'um. Oldest boy is with the Marines. Just like his old man, I guess."

"My son is . . . ." Wainwright let his voice trail off. "He's a wonderful boy."

"Good for him."

They arrived in Dawes and Wainwright directed him to his home. Bud pulled into the driveway. The truck's headlights lit up the front of the house.

"Can I offer you some money?" Wainwright asked. "For your trouble?" Where would he get it? From the back of the toilet?

Bud looked at the house and then back at Wainwright. "No trouble at all, Chief. Hey, wait a minute." He opened a compartment in the big armrest next to his thigh. "Here, take this." He handed Wainwright a boxed pumpkin pie.

"I couldn't."

"Oh, cripes. The missus got ten pies waitin' for me. Was gonna give it to my mother, but the nurse told me she wouldn't eat it. Go ahead. You share it with your boy."

Wainwright feared if he thanked him again it would make him look like a pathetic vagabond, so he merely nodded and got out of the truck.

"You gonna be able to get a ride tomorrow to pick up your car?" Bud called to him. "I got the day off, so if you want I'll come up and give you a lift."

"No . . . no. That won't be necessary. Thank you so much." The situation demanded he use those words again.

"Happy Thanksgiving, Chief. Have a good one."

"And the same to you and your family." Wainwright watched the Dodge drive off into the night.

Inside, he found a crusty spoon in the sink and headed for the Soloflex. He stepped over a skirmish line of empty soup cans, sat down and began eating the pumpkin pie. There was no taste, no satisfaction of hunger, just the mechanical action of feeding himself. He felt suspended from the ceiling on hair thin wires. He wanted to cry but all the tears were gone.

A moment of absolute clarity struck him then, for the first time since the world was young.

It brought no bitter disappointment, no sense of failure. Things had turned out for the best, turned out as they were intended. Destiny's hand does not waver.

He was no murderer.

That particular broken bottle wasn't stuck in his foot. The poor cat might disagree, but he was never going to harm a man and his wife as they sat down to a good and simple meal justly earned.

He may have fallen through the elevator doors and down the rabbit hole, but he was no murderer. Never had been. Never would be.

He had been a teacher.

He had been a soldier.

He had been a husband and a father.

Dear God, how I miss you both.

He had been a good man once.

He had been.

Waves of nausea rose from his stomach, curtailing his thoughts. The pie was half gone. More food — more sugar — than he'd eaten in a long time. He left the rest on the Soloflex and went to bed.

On his way up the stairs, his bowel rebelled and deposited a load in his trousers before he could make the toilet.

THE NEXT AFTERNOON, after a long, hard morning of doing nothing, Wainwright bathed himself for the first time since the job interview at Blythewood. Lacking shampoo, he washed his hair with a few drops of dish detergent gleaned from a depleted plastic bottle in the kitchen.

Why he chose this time of day he didn't know. It might mean something. Or perhaps the time had come and nothing more. He toweled off and went into his bedroom. The .45 rested on the mattress. He sat next to it. For the briefest instant he considered putting on his dress blues but decided against it. No more dishonor would be heaped on the uniform.

Naked we come into this world and naked we must leave it.

Wainwright picked up the pistol and tried to fit it in his mouth. The cold metal banged painfully against his brittle teeth and made him gag. That wouldn't do. He pressed the wet muzzle against his right temple and summoned all his remaining courage.

Breath left him. An infinite stretch of perfect stillness cleared his dim eyes. He fancied he could see right through the walls of the old house on into the distance.

The rotary phone on the nightstand jangled. A second after. A second before.

Wainwright's head turned mechanically and he stared at the telephone for the length of five rings. Then he shifted the .45 to his left hand and picked up the handset.

"Hello?"

It was Jennifer from Kilburn School. She asked him if he had a nice Thanksgiving and profusely apologized for not getting back to him sooner. He listened to everything she said, thanked her at the end and hung up the phone.

Wainwright laid the .45 back in the box and stood up. Eyes, big as lighthouse reflectors, swept the bedroom, held on the Linden Triple Chime. On new legs he wobbled over to the clock and carefully brushed away cobwebs and dust and a wolf spider or two from the mahogany case. With the palm of his hand he wiped the glass clean. It was a beautiful thing still: the graceful lines, the silvered dial and brass accents. A fine piece, he thought. German made. Well worth the money.

He set its hands by instinct and a guess. He wound the key.

The sweep stirred and resumed the march of seconds and minutes and hours.

Lightheadedness overcame him. It seemed to emanate from somewhere in his temple. He massaged the area with two fingertips to assure himself there was no damage, no hole. A peculiar notion tugged at the corners of his cracked lips.

He looked down at the clock's face and without hope of an answer asked, "Am I here?"

Another Girl

Mr. McInroy claims to be familiar with various addictions, Norse goddesses on motorcycles, and the allure of each. He adamantly asserts that the divine is always with us, whether riding a chariot across the sky, hanging from a cross, or driving the back roads of America in a Dodge Charger Hellcat. His title is stolen from a Stones lyric, his desert land from his novel Army Girl as well as a forthcoming and as yet untitled book which continues with some of the same themes and characters.

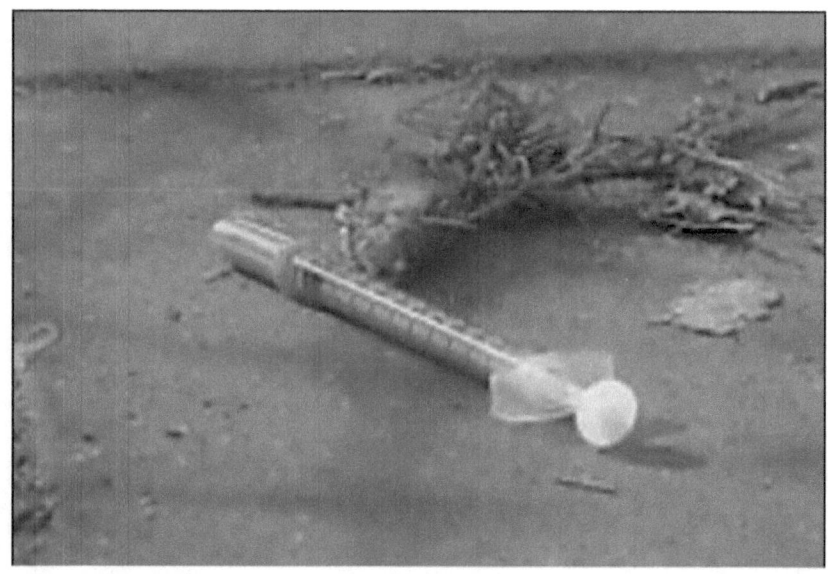

Another Girl

J S McInroy

The mileage turns one eleven. The diamondblack Hellcat RT slips around the tight righthand curve as efficiently as ever it might have were Junior Johnson or Number 3 at the wheel. For an old man Dad still has his mojo. Half a second ahead stands a forlorn hiker in the dew damp morning. No higher than his right hip his thumb juts out.

Father eases the gas a bit. Ever the hopeful child, the Son asks, "We gonna stop fer 'im?"

"No," Father replies. "He's not waiting for us. And please, if it's not too much trouble, can the NASCAR accent. We're not from South Carolina. This is way north of there."

"Jes feels raaght," Son drawls. "Anaways, wha not? We've picked up wos'n thisun on jes a whim, and this guy looks 'bout as mizbral'z y'all kin git."

"Want to find yourself out there beside him? Your last little adventure of the kind didn't end so well. At least as I remember. This one's not in any kind of good place. But he's exactly where he needs to be. Just like you were."

By this time the Dodge is a mile down the road, and only the memory of the hiker remains between them.

"He looks unhappy," sighs the Son.

"And so he is," asserts Father. "But so what? Jeremy Bentham was an idiot. Happiness is for fools, and unless old Jer was a cynic of my own magnitude, his advocacy of such brands him as the greatest fool of all. Without pain, pleasure is impossible and vice versa. Thus it may be asserted that, for some at least, the sole purpose of pleasure is to make possible the experience of

175

pain, while the pain then becomes the source of that human being's awareness of pleasure, which, in turn...."

"*Enough,*" *groans the Son. "What's this heap got fer music?*"

"She's beautiful," Dean exclaims, his left leg beginning to stiffen, his shorter limb to ache just a bit. The object of his wounded enchantment could only be the Norse Sjofn arriving on a Japanese motorcycle. The ride is black as are her jacket and full-face helmet. Her legs are Levi blue. The bike purrs into a uey. The goddess nods.

Dean's companion, Kenny Babbs, lifts a casual hand. "Siri," he exclaims and with one word claims the vision as his own.

It must be the oxy. Dean is fully aware of himself. Of his obvious physical and social defects. But something calls. From within? From without? Her. The glacier shudders. A calf is born. The black occlusion of her helmet slips away. From it falls the golden sunshine of endless summers in the park. No park particular. No time. Golden Gate happened too many lives ago.

Dean's leg really aches. His broken wrist too. His butt.

The woman, the supernatural being of time before memory's inception, is beside him. Between him and Babbs. Her essence slips and curls itself somniferus within them.

"Hey, Kenny," she breathes through ivory teeth. Red lips bloody as the northern sun. "Good to see ya." Turning to Dean, looking straight into him with eyes of polar blaze. White they are as only the bluest of blue eyes can be. Unwavering, she asks behind her, "Who's yer friend?"

Babbs, "Dean."

Dean's own eyes are brown, this day wound about with crimson vines, rimmed in circles of cartoon red. His teeth, crooked as her gaze is straight, are also brown. Darker even than his eyes.

Crack.

No more.

Straight as time's arrow he is. Doesn't even drink. His mother is suggesting implants. She said to wait three years. It's been two and a half. Maybe....

"Seem to be banged up a bit," Siri jabs. "Best ta pay for whacha smoke."

"That's not it," Babbs interjects. "Deano got hit by some teenager texting or something. Just turned right in front of him."

THE TIME, AS must every time, becomes another. Siri checks a man's watch. She will fly. To a doctor of some indefinite calling. Must be a Gyno.

Dean attempts to fashion visions of her. Sjofn, according to some, the almighty alter-hugr of Frigga herself, her legs, inviting and adorably askew, imprisoned by iron stirrups, the darkness of her immortal self exposed to the ravenous medico.

Him.

Dean.

He fails. Hers is not to be so easily constrained or contained. Sjofn or Siri. She is no one's playtoy.

His pain becomes intense, his vision as redrimmed as his eyes. Her cycle purrs constrained energy. Another uey. Siri is gone. The sun may be warming the patio beneath them —he can taste the salt of the beads on Kenny's forehead — but Dean has been frozen. A king crab not quite dead, he is reviving only to be eaten. His oxy is almost gone. There's hydro back home. 750's. A mess of them. They may kill his soul. He does not fear they will.

They're the shits for pain.

"Gotta go," he mumbles, fumbles for keys. Jerks the old Ford into reverse. Is out of the steamer and into the whining AC of the 99 Taurus.

He only has six oxys left. At a cost of four dollars each they were a good deal. But Billy has disappeared as has Marge. There is no more anywhere. Even at ten bucks a pop. What the almighty hell? He gulps four.

MONTREAL. CITY OF his birth and early childhood. "American" the kids in whateveritwas that passed for progressive kindergarten there and then had named him. And when he returned alone with Mom to the states? "Frenchie" was the disparaging term of the day until, older and wiser by a year, the others began calling him a frog.

Dean soon accepted his fate and went the way of many outsiders of the early grades. Withdrawing into the comfortable gloom of himself, the world he chose to live in revolved around one Dean M. Holmes, the hyperactive — oft confirmed, oft rejected diagnosis — offspring of a sunshine mother who followed the Dead, often with son in arms, until Jerry's unfortunate demise at which point she retreated within the vaporous shell of cannabis and an occasional fling with the ecstasy of ecstasy while all that time growing ever more successful as a patent attorney with her own lucrative shingle. She worked from home, stayed stoned at home, and eventually schooled her son. At home and all alone.

A better than best friend, a holistic healer no less, advised her concerning the boy's natural enthusiasm. "Nurture the energy," he whispered, inserting himself between Mom's legs and up into the place from whence Dean had sprung. "Allow it free rein." And then, as they faced each other connected, he continued her instruction as to the pleasure/pain continuum, imprinting bright images of one of these upon her breasts with the end of the blunt from which he toked himself into cosmic awareness of the other.

Dean had discovered her diaries, had caught glimpses of her speckled mammaries, and had dug his own continuum from the careless discards of his mother's journey toward enlightenment. He read Tom Wolfe, lived within the chords and lyrics of a music before his time, and grew toward the delicate gypsy biker he was destined to become. Leaving nothing but childhood behind, he remained an innocent partaker of the complex pleasures and pains of his imagination. Augmented of course by both crack and meth. Ecstasy as well, but that just blew around the coliseum of his mind like the cheers of circus goers crazed by their own lusts and fears.

Mom caught him before he had used heroin anything more than maybe half or possibly a dozen times. Mom freaked.

So off to rehab and into the bland state of his current recovery.

Thank you, Abbot Labs. Without Vicodin in its many forms, he would have been left abandoned. Descended into a hell of no possible exit. As anyone who knows anything knows, however, such pale approximations such as Vike and oxy, and the whole opioid family offer no true salvation. Theirs is a purgatory of longing for the bliss only Lady H is able to offer. But, at least in purgatory dwells hope of some higher order. In the big H one hopes no more. Except for more of the hell he's already going through. The only cure for the suffering is that which has caused the pain. Dean dearly loved his Lady H, and she would willingly have become his harsh mistress, blistering her own rosebuds upon his pale skin even as her song set every nerve in his body aflame and moved his consciousness to a dark but most comfortable place where the outside world was illusion, its population pygmies babbling about their fallen towers.

Mom had put a halt to such delusion, had turned him away from the horror heroin addiction usually becomes. She had set him on the straight and narrow. Had even bought him a new bike once he finished his thirty days. He needed it. To get to all those damn meetings. He could have afforded it on his own. His grandmother had left him a trust fund. But Mom wanted to be as much a part of his recovery as is possible for one not herself addicted.

Not that he is an addict. He hadn't used enough heroin for that particular appellation to apply. But his is a long and almost profound relationship with several of the other demons in the rogues' gallery of rehab and NA. He is, they assured him, definitely an addict. They almost convinced him. But really. Except for the irregular use —one or two pops a day— of one of the wannabes, he has stayed clean and sober. Well almost. Functional for sure.

He'd best stay away from meetings for a while though. The humorless assholes — well-meaning as such assholes might be — are downright blind to certain needs. He's had an accident, for fuck's sake. And he needs the script the doctor has given him. Legal and prescribed. But they'd piss and moan, accuse him of slip slidin' down some slippery slope. Of not really trying to get straight. Of sabotaging his own recovery. Oh yeah! He was responsible for the stupid bitch turning into him?

But then...? He does need the shit, just like they say. And he likes it too. Just like they say. Best to stay away for a bit. The pious pissheads can really freak a guy out. Lucky, him running into Kenny. Kenny is cool. And he's got nothing against a drop of whiskey or a toke or two. Or even, Dean would bet, a snort of something better than glue. Yeah. Kenny's the future. And Siri too. That chick rules.

TWO WHITE BEAUTIES washed with bottled water as he drives. Two more when he gets home.

Sleep. No perchances present.

To darkness he awakes. A sliver of something pale slides beneath the door. Sleep again.

Summer mornings are too bright way too early. He is conscious of the blazing blood inscribed 4:36 upon the face of his bedside alarm. He twists. He turns. Spirals again to no avail.

Taking himself in hand he begins a calming ritual and before he knows he again dozes. This time between muddy sheets.

The blood-drawn numbers scream 6:46. He is as stiff as his linen. There is no return to sleep. He has dreamed. Of Siri. She awaits his call. There will be time. There is time. The rest of the Hydro. Sleep is always possible.

Siri is again his dream. But circumstances have changed. She stands, helmet in hand, leather slipped open upon a yellow almost green sweater of some most erotic fabric. With her are two companions of more traditional attire. Shorts. Halter tops. One in ankle wrapped sandals. The other flip-flopped and cross legged where she stands. They are talking. And laughing his way. Siri glances over more often than do they. He would approach but something holds him back.

There exists a barrier. Not material. Not energy. Stronger than either. Either they or he is in a bubble. A membrane of such capacity that it contains all of everything they are or he is. Past, present, future, and never was, is or will be. Maybe the bubbles touch. Possibly both he and they are enclosed in separate envelopes of insubstance. He does not know. He cannot know. But there they stand as though he were just across a most ordinary room. He hears the murmur of their mingled voices. He is able to approach but not touch. He reaches out. His hand disappears. He calls to her. His voice will not carry. Siri looks his way and smiles.

Sad or scornful? He cannot say. The others lift delicate fingers to painted clownmouths, their titters unmuffled derision. They are mummers in drag. He knows that to them he is the clown. An old saw of his mother's twirls about his ears, catches up in his hair. "East is East, and West is West, and never the twain shall meet." Is he East or West? He cannot answer. But it matters not. His mother's words ring untrue.

Siri approaches.

Halts.

The barrier keeps them inches and light years apart. Her consciousness, however, is not bound. She enters his mind. Communicates.

AFTERNOON. HE MAY never sleep again. At least this day. No mere dream could have spoken so profoundly, have twisted the life like soiled wash water from his soul. Siri can be no Sjofin. But, Dean knows she is. The goddess has spoken not in words, images or anything tangible. She has overwhelmed him with his own images of himself and then, without comment, slipped into non-rem imperception. He has become his own mirror. He despairs. Awake or asleep, dreaming or later-on awake, he cannot escape the image his reflected self beheld of the gnocchi-blob of his soft physicality. To employ a young woman's word. He finds himself gross.

His ears. One lies flat against his skull; the other curled out at its upper margin. One eye stares noticeably wider than the other; one cheekbone might actually be seen as missing, his lower jaw so undershot that a clinically minded observer would be led to question his ability to bite off a hunk of anything more resistant than an overboiled potato. And of course, his teeth. Had he been consuming oatmeal, brown sugar, and molasses the viewing image might have found a plausible explanation for the color of his teeth. And were there some hidden but very real flaw in the looking glass, of which the reflective observer were aware, then perhaps their contradictory lines and ragged edges might be overlooked. But the only flaws are his. His teeth are not simply brown and misaligned. They are simply ugly. As is he.

The mirror also views him naked. He is dressed, he would swear. But up and down his chest straggle remnants of extinguished smokes. Some bright and immediate. Others soft and brown as his teeth. On his legs too. And one or two upon his scrotum. Thank providence or whatever is out there that his view

182

is only full-frontal. He has heard Mom being spanked. Has felt the belt himself. His B side no doubt sports a welt or more. Ugly bruises ring his wrists and ankles, results of moments spent imagining past whatever his ears have heard.

His belly waxes pregnant beneath the concave arc of his chest. His knees are juts of overcooked turkey bone, his feet narrow and flat, his toes too short for the name. He could be hooved. Or so he thinks.

Siri left him with the echo of a high song of love, "*Himlen Runt Hornet*," he might have heard her sing, but the words made no sense to him, and before he could even be sure they were words, Siri/Sjofin was no more. His memory of himself though has been etched upon the insubstantial face of his soul.

Awakening to a fading afternoon is rarely a moment of clarity. Such is the case for Dean. He isn't sure where he is or where he might have been. He does seem to be inside himself looking out upon the visible portions of his body, his skinny legs and gray, blue-knotted arms. He would have taken no significant notice of the fact that he is clad in dark and light blue checked boxers and an old and comfortable Black Oak Arkansas tee shirt were it not for the fact that he is certain he should have been naked. Or is that the other way around? In which case his summer weight garb should have been expected.

One thing for certain. He needs a shower. He smells like a spicy mixture of stale urine and Arabaca beans. Cupping his hand to his pale lips, he gags at the odor of his decomposing breath. First he will give his teeth a good brushing and swallow some Listerine. Sometimes he can't stand himself.

The mirror. The dream. The giggling girls. The lethal icicle, Siri! Paste drools from the tube, spittle from a stroker's toothless gums. He has forgotten until he sees his mirrored face from out the viewports of his own awareness. Two red splotches something like branded Kaposis' decorate either side of his underjaw. Not the result of his own ministrations, they are two of the lesser effects of his accident. However there they smolder, red, black rimmed, and terminal. Just as the girls had found so amusing, and as Siri has shown him. He is a disgrace to himself, to humanity. Ugly unto death.

He will never have the frozen goddess. Will never find even an unappetizing member of the opposite sex with whom to bond. His memories and fantasies of Mom are the best he will ever get. She will never leave him. Her love ignores crooked teeth and blatant sores. She will be his forever. And he will be hers.

NO BATH, NO oral hygiene. Dean falls back into bed. Finds an embracing darkness. Once again imagines himself his mother. Once again sleeps within the comfort of his own yellow ejaculation. *Himlen Runt Hornet* slips softly about the bare walls, clambers up the slats of his windowblind, and falls upon his intertwined form from the popcorn ceiling. The common time for sleeping comes and goes. Dean awakes at a standard workingman's hour. 6:00AM. The sun shines; the music has grown silent. He lies and watches morning's fleeting clouds at play with the maple leaves outside projected upon a far wall. His mind is blank. Mom clatters past. Her Smart Car starts. Holistic Hal is at a conference. Dean is alone. The day is his to create as he will, but his goddamn wrist aches, his leg is on fire, only the empty vessels of once prescribed relief await his reach.

As if it were time — and it is — the bedside alarm blares on: QBX, Capitalland's Voice of classic rock is broadcasting music for a change. The Stones "Dead Flowers"? Just perfect! He's wide awake at 6:34 in the AM with no Susie, no familiarity with silk chairs or Kentucky Derbies. He's just another dead-ass posy, or at least the guy who gets bunches of them every stinking day of his rotten life. Alone, unaccompanied by even the raggediest of companions. Alone in a slightly below-grade split-level room without even the works, let alone the much beloved *other girl.* No Siri she. Oh, so much better. And he can have her. Kenny will bring her along even if he doesn't use.

"Fuck you, Siri," he hawks into his empty chest. "I don't need no one but myself and Lady H. Fuck you."

His phone is dead, but past-tense Mom keeps a land line. Kenny'll recognize the number. And before too long H will ease his pain all the hell away. Dean brightens into all possibility....

At least for such as he.

Shale ledge slivering itself into clay. Dusted with wind-borne shards of keen desert sand from below. Some drifted over, some of recent deposit, bent, spent, and fragmented vials, needleshafts, spoons, rubbery tourniquets, and a Zippo of ancient lineage. A tiny pile of unwrapped but unused tampons has gathered dust to its absorbent self. Two pair of flip-flops, one pink, the other abraded clean of color.

Above, the sky stretches cloudless, sunless, dazzling. Off into an unknowable distance and direction empty sand stretches to a vanishing point in no manner suggestive of a horizon. Either this world is of immense diameter or is flat, a layer rather than the comfortably self-contained yet interactive orb we know as earth.

A black circle of recent creation speaks of fire. Words scratched pale white upon ghostly gray fade into mystery.

"Mar _," S_ _i," "Ru _h," "F _ _ _ _you _AM" is all left to be puzzled over. Except, that is, for the overdrawn, over and over, drawn again and again arrow. It points straight away. Across the sand. Toward...?

The Hellcat purrs into a spot beside a lake. Erie. Buffalo looms north, Erie and Cleveland to the south and west. The desert place is nowhere in this land.

It is everywhere.

"The Farthest West Beach" is a story of many layers, at the heart of which lies an ineffable truth, itself subject to unraveling. Perhaps the best characterization is that all we know is deception, and that may not be so terrible, for what we come to understand over the course of our maturing into young adulthood borders both upon the tragic and the absurd. Mattina learns much and so does the reader this day at the beach. We all swim with her into deep water toward distant rocks, and those upon whom we once depended remain ashore, afraid to follow.

The Farthest West Beach

Maria Palmara

Mattina hated sitting in the middle. The thirteen-year-old sat trapped in the backseat of her father's '62 Olds between her brother Jack and Ah Zee, the aunt from Italy who always sat next to the door because of the trouble with her leg.

Every few minutes, Mattina lifted her head to look over the front seat through the windshield beyond her parents, Carmine and Sugar, and the baby, Rose, who was asleep on the front seat between them. But from where Mattina sat, she could only see a small strip of the dull gray highway ahead.

It was early morning and the pale sunlight was beginning to creep into the car. They had left the city before dawn to beat the traffic out on the Island, but now they were behind schedule because they had to stop at the Chevron so Sugar could change Rose, who had wet right through her plastic pants.

They were going to Aunt Baby and Uncle Sal's summer party. This year, they were having it on a beach they had never been to. At dinner the night before, Carmine complained about the drive.

"It's too far," he said, as he cut into his Saturday night steak. "Way the hell out. It's enough to get to their house as it is. Now we have to drive even more?" Carmine was always against his younger brother's move from the city to open up a TV repair shop near the shore, especially since he had offered to bring him into the laborers' union. But the dinner conversation shifted to Jack when he announced that he wasn't going with them to the beach. For a moment, when Mattina heard that Jack wasn't going, she thought she'd stay home with him even though he was four years older.

"You're not staying home and hanging out with those beatnik friends of yours," Carmine had said, pointing his fork at Jack. "A Sunday with your family ain't gonna kill you."

But now as they were driving, Mattina was getting excited about the beach the way she used to when she was younger. She sat up and leaned over the front seat and spotted a few sea gulls circling in the distance. Maybe it wouldn't be so bad, she thought. Once they were there, maybe she would be able to slip away for a while and spend time with her twin cousins, Cindy and Mindy.

"What are you jumping around back there for?" Carmine spoke to Mattina through the rearview mirror.

"I'm just looking," she said to the reflection of his little brown eyes.

"Well, sit back. We'll be there in a few minutes."

Sugar turned around. "You're not getting carsick, are you?" she asked. "You should have eaten something before we left."

Mattina saw a tiny image of herself in her mother's white-rimmed sunglasses. "I'm all right," she said, and sank back down between Ah Zee and Jack, who was curled up next to the door pretending to be asleep.

Mattina looked out the side window past Ah Zee, who sat like a statue as she stared ahead. The woman's profile was framed by the blur of the white sand dunes and wild beach shrubs passing behind her. The mole above her lip was a perfect pink knot. Her black hair was wound tight into a ball, the black sweater she always wore was buttoned up to the collar, and her long black skirt covered most of her brace and special shoe with the thick sole.

Ah Zee was Sugar's aunt, the last member of that side of the family to come over. When Ah Zee's husband died two years ago, she came to this country to live with Mattina's grandmother. And when Mattina's grandmother died last year, Ah Zee came to live with them. She couldn't go back to Italy alone, both Carmine and Sugar agreed. Not without a husband.

As they continued along the highway, the air inside the car began to heat up. Mattina could already feel that it was going to be a hot day and wondered how Ah Zee could stand it in that long skirt and sweater. She looked down at her own pale arms and legs and wished that she had worn long pants and a long-sleeved shirt, instead of shorts and Jack's white baggy tee.

"Does anybody want a Lifesaver?" Sugar asked as she rummaged through her beach bag.

Ah Zee leaned forward. "*Voglio*," she said, quickly stopping herself, shaking her head in frustration with the language. "Yes. I want," she said clearly. Mattina took the candy from her mother, unwrapped one, and gave it to Ah Zee, who immediately chewed the mint to bits.

When Carmine turned onto the beach road, Mattina grabbed the top of the front seat again and pulled herself up. This time she saw the iron blue ocean spread out flat and wide beyond the soft sand dunes.

"You see that boat out there?" Carmine spoke to them all as he gestured to one of the barges on the horizon. "Ah Zee, you see that? See it, Jack? Can you see that Tina?"

Mattina hated it when he called her Tina, but she turned and looked past her mother's head to see the ships. Ah Zee managed an affirmative sound. Jack, who was still curled on his side, buried his head deeper into his arms.

"When I was in the Navy," Carmine began, "we'd dive right off the deck. Me...Radio Joe...Billy Doughnuts. We never got caught," he said. "Swim all around the boat and then sneak back by climbing up the anchor chain." Mattina looked out at the enormous ships and began to wonder how it was possible to climb up an anchor chain.

"We have to turn here," Sugar said, cutting Carmine's story short as she read from a small piece of paper. "Baby said it's the last beach on the west side."

"I'm telling you there ain't nothing out this way," Carmine said as he made the wide turn and headed west toward the desolate beaches. "I don't see why we had to come way out here. Are you sure

189

she said west? Who knows with you writing down directions? Right, Zee?" Carmine looked through the rearview mirror to try and get Ah Zee's attention. "Who knows with her?" he said again, raising his eyebrows and nodding his head in Sugar's direction.

"I'm sure," Sugar insisted. "She said the west side."

"I just said you never know with you, that's all. Right, Zee?" Carmine sat up and strained to make eye contact with the aunt through the narrow mirror, but she just kept looking out the side window.

Carmine gave up on getting Ah Zee to join him in his little joke about Sugar when he spotted Jack, who had slid down in his seat and now had his arms crossed over his face. "Eh, Jack?" Carmine's playful tone disappeared as he called to his son. "Jack. I'm talking to you."

Jack slowly unfolded his arms and straightened up in the seat. "I was sleeping," he said, brushing his long hair off his forehead and leaning into the armrest. He opened the small silver ashtray cover on the door handle and then snapped it shut. "But I still don't see why I had to come."

"Don't start with that again," Carmine said, raising his voice and sitting up to look back at Jack through the mirror. Mattina braced herself for another fight between them. They were always fighting. About his friends, his hair, his grades at school. She hated it when they fought, but was grateful that it was Jack who was always the focus of their father's anger.

"Carmine, be quiet," Sugar said, patting Rose who began to stir and grunt. "You're gonna wake her up."

Carmine glanced down at the baby. "A day at the beach is good for yous all," he said in a softer voice. "The air out here is good." He was again speaking to everyone in the car. "Yous all gotta breathe a lot when you're out here. Right, Zee? Everybody breathe," he said as he rolled open all four electric windows from the control pad on the driver's door.

The cold morning air rushed into the car like an assault.

Mattina's long brown hair flew into her face. She quickly pulled it back and began braiding it into a thick cord. Ah Zee pulled her kerchief up from around her sweater and tied it tightly under her chin. Jack slid down in his seat again, crossed his arms, and curled back on his side. Rose woke up screaming. Sugar immediately closed her window. When Carmine saw that the baby was awake, he closed the other three.

"Now see what you did?" Sugar said as she picked up Rose and seated her on her lap.

"How's my little piss clam?" Carmine said, reaching over and pinching his daughter's chubby leg, making her scream even louder.

Sugar bounced the baby on her knee and fluffed her damp curls. Rose was the image of Carmine. Even at three, everyone commented that her little nose was destined to become Roman like her father's. People used to say that Mattina took after Carmine, but not so much anymore.

The morning sun followed them along the horizon. Mattina tied off the end of her braid with a small rubber band and sat as still she could so there wouldn't be any more trouble. The air in the car was heating up again, and she could feel the back of her legs sticking to the leatherette seats. She had her bathing suit on under her clothes and the elastic trim was digging into her skin. At the last minute while getting dressed that morning, she had put on her navy blue tank even though she had already decided that she wasn't going into the water. She remembered their beach trip the summer before and how all the people stared when Carmine kept waving to her from the shore shouting that she was drifting too far out.

"There's Sal's car!" Sugar pointed ahead as they turned into the last parking lot on the west side.

"Another new Caddy?" Carmine said, as he drove toward the 1968 sky blue convertible. "Jesus. Could he of found a spot further out? That sign says the beach ain't even open."

Carmine pulled up close to the curb so that Ah Zee wouldn't have to walk too far. Then, he and Jack got out and began unpacking the car. Sugar got out, cinched her aquamarine cover up, hoisted Rose onto her hip with one arm, and with the other opened the back door and helped Ah Zee. Mattina slid out after and slipped her arm around her aunt's.

"Ain't this great," Uncle Sal said, walking up from the beach, his white tank hanging loosely over his Hawaiian print shorts. "We got the whole place to ourselves."

Uncle Sal was a younger, thinner version of Carmine. His curly black hair had not yet begun to recede and gray. Following closely behind him were two teenage boys, wearing only cut-off jeans. Their bodies were wiry and tanned. One had shaggy blonde hair that kept falling over his eyes, and the other was taller and wearing wire-rimmed sunglasses which were too big for his head. Mattina thought they made him look like a giant fly.

"Here, let the kids carry those," Sal said as he grabbed a case of Schlitz from Carmine and handed it to the boy with the shaggy blonde hair. The taller boy took the case of soda from the trunk.

Carmine watched the two boys suspiciously as they walked away. "Who are those guys?" he said, tucking his Banlon shirt into his baggy work pants.

"They're kids that work for me on Saturdays. At the shop. I told you I can't keep up with all the work out here."

The two boys walked by Mattina, who stood unnoticed, as she steadied Ah Zee. Uncle Sal grabbed the chest of food, Carmine shouldered the other case of beer, and Jack carried the rest of the bags and the umbrella.

Aunt Baby and Uncle Sal's friends had already arrived. They had brought long folding tables and benches and arranged them under a large tarp. Some of the women brought pans and kitchen utensils and stood over barbecues frying sausage and ham. Most of the men were sitting having coffee. A few had already started drinking beer. Uncle Sal had his eight-track hooked up to a car battery, and a Frank Sinatra tape was blasting.

"You found us!" Aunt Baby squealed as she came rushing over

to greet them. "Sal, lower that thing," she shouted over the music.

Aunt Baby helped Sugar and Mattina set up a beach chair for Ah Zee. Jack set up the umbrella next to her and then spread out the blankets. When he finished, he unrolled a towel a few yards away, took off his sneakers, and stretched out face down.

They were at the last developed beach on the strip. To the west, lay miles of untouched shore, with massive jagged rocks clustered along the edge. Mattina sat down on the blanket and watched the seagulls hovering above as the waves crashed into the dark towers, creating airy pastel ribbons in the spray.

"Mattina! How are you?" Aunt Baby said, walking up to her holding a bottle of Fresca. Her straw blonde hair was tied back and her gold chain glittered against her dark tan. The yellow and green muu-muu she wore had yellow and green muu-muus printed on it. "The girls are down there," she said, and pointed to the shore with the bottle.

Mattina looked down the beach and saw her cousins who were near the water with the two boys in cut-off jeans and two other boys. It looked like they were playing volleyball but without a net, just a line drawn in the sand. Carmine was deep into a conversation at the tables, and Sugar had started frying eggs in a pan over a barbecue. They had brought a thin clothesline and tied Rose to Ah Zee's beach chair, so she wouldn't wander off. The baby was sitting in the sand digging a hole with her yellow plastic shovel. It would have been the perfect opportunity to get away, but Jack was still pretending to be asleep on his towel. If Mattina left now, Ah Zee would be alone watching Rose.

"No. I'll stay up here for a while," she said.

"Okay, Sweetheart." Aunt Baby gave her niece a quick kiss on her forehead before she walked back to the tables.

Mattina sat down on the blanket, leaned back on her elbows, and watched the game, which consisted of the boys chasing the girls into the water and then falling over each other. The twins were both wearing bikinis. Cindy's was bright orange, and Mindy's was bright yellow. Even though they were a year younger than Mattina, they were taller, thinner, and somehow seemed older. They had the kind of skin that tanned golden, not like hers which quickly burned and peeled. Their straight black hair was long and worn loose. Mattina thought about unbraiding hers, but knew how wild it could get, especially on the beach.

"*Vai*," Ah Zee said, who had been watching Mattina. "Go," she said again, nodding to the group.

"It's all right. I don't want to yet."

Sugar walked over to drop off the fried egg sandwiches she just made. "Here," she said handing the plate to her daughter. "I made yours Egyptian."

Egyptian eggs used to be Mattina's favorite. When she was little, she used to love to pull out the doughy middle of the thick slices of Italian bread and watch as her mother put each piece in a hot pan of butter and then carefully crack an egg into the centers. They hadn't made those together in years. Mattina looked down at the overcooked egg encased in the fried crust and thought it looked like an enormous eye staring back at her.

Rose had completely tangled the clothesline around Ah Zee's beach chair. Mattina got up, freed her sister, and handed her the egg sandwich. The baby immediately pulled the yolk out of its socket, threw it in the sand, and began gnawing on the greasy bread. Mattina handed a sandwich to Ah Zee, who neatly folded a paper napkin around the bottom and nibbled at the top as she gazed into the ocean.

It took a while for her cousins to notice that Mattina had arrived, but when they finally did, Mindy ran up to the blanket. As her cousin came toward her, Mattina thought that she looked like the model in the Coppertone ad.

"How long have you been here?" Mindy said, falling to her knees in the sand, her dark skin dripping salt water. "Come down."

"I'm gonna stay here a while," Mattina said, and looked over at Rose who was now burying the rest of the sandwich.

"Come on," Mindy insisted, grabbed Mattina's arm, and pulled until she finally got up and followed her down the beach. "We're playing volleyball. You know like we always play," she said as she dragged Mattina behind her.

"Hey, Tina!" Carmine was standing and calling over three rows of tables. "Where you going?"

Mattina stopped and broke free from Mindy's grip. "Just down there," she said and pointed to the four boys who had encircled Cindy.

"Who are those guys?" she heard Carmine ask her uncle.

"I told you. They work at the shop. And a couple of their friends. They're just kids, Carm."

"They're good boys," Aunt Baby said.

"A little old, ain't they?"

"They're okay. Relax." Uncle Sal slid another beer in his brother's direction.

"Why don't you stay up here and help your mother with the baby?" Carmine shouted down to Mattina.

"No," Ah Zee called in her niece's direction. "*Vai*," she said, again, waving her thin arm toward the water.

Carmine sat back down, pulled the beer tab, and threw it into the sand. "This is why I drink," he said, causing a few weak laughs at the table.

As she approached the group, Mattina knew they all had heard. A fat pale boy nodded in her direction. The other boys fidgeted in their spots.

"Play on our side," Cindy said, pulling Mattina between her and a red-headed boy with a dog tooth. The boy with the shaggy blonde hair, stood behind her. Mattina turned around, and he smiled at her.

"Come on already," the boy with the wire-rimmed sunglasses shouted from across the line.

Mattina looked at her cousins in their bright bikinis, dark tans, and long silky hair. She still had on her shorts and Jack's big white tee, which was billowing out in the sea breeze like the sails on the small boats off shore.

Once the game started, Mattina realized that they were not playing by the rules she knew. They were just going to continue to fool around the way they had been. Whenever the ball went to Cindy or Mindy, they'd tap it so lightly that it couldn't make it across the line. If one of the twins caught the ball, one of the boys would tackle her, and they would both go tumbling into the surf, laughing. Mattina wondered why her cousins were playing this way. When they played together last summer, they had been fierce. But now it seemed like the girls weren't even trying to win. After a while, Mattina also found herself laughing at their poor playing.

Occasionally, the ball would fly past Mattina, and she'd swing an arm out in a half-hearted attempt to hit it. The boys continued to give their full attention to the twins, and the twins were too involved with the boys to notice that their cousin was left out until Cindy finally yelled to throw the ball to Mattina.

The boy with the shaggy blonde hair tapped the ball to her, but before Mattina could hit it, the boy with the wire-rimmed sunglasses crossed over the line and grabbed her around the waist. "You're going down," he said, and pulled her into the surf with him.

The others started laughing, so Mattina started laughing too even though his grip was hurting her. "You're not going anywhere," he said, holding her in place. As she struggled to push his hands away from her sides, she looked up the beach and saw the short, wide figure of her father stomping toward them.

"What the hell's going on?"

For a moment, Mattina didn't recognize Carmine, who had changed into his tan plaid swimming trunks. The boy with the wire-rimmed sunglasses immediately released her.

"Come're," Carmine yelled. "Now."

"We're just playing, Uncle Carmine," Mindy said, cheerfully.

"Well, that's enough playing."

"I just fell," Mattina said, getting up and wiping the wet sand from Jack's tee.

"Go back and sit with your aunt."

"Sorry," the boy with the wire-rimmed sunglasses said, not looking in Carmine's direction.

"Listen, *Sorry,*" Carmine said, taking a step closer and pointing to all the boys. "I don't want to see any of yous around my daughter again. You hear? The game's over." He trudged back up to the picnic tables, his short legs kicking up bits of sand behind him.

The twins gave Mattina a sympathetic look as they watched her walk back to the blanket. Then, they turned and followed the boys, who were walking farther down the beach.

When Carmine sat back down, Aunt Baby playfully slapped him on the shoulder. "You are an over-protective father," she said.

"What am I supposed to do? Sit and watch while that bird's got his hands on my daughter?"

"They're just kids," Uncle Sal said. "They're just fooling around."

"Never mind. She can sit up here for a while," Carmine said, and took a long swig of beer.

Mattina sat back down on the blankets and looked down the shore at the dark jagged rocks. Thin watery ribbons of green and blue appeared and then faded above them as the seagulls scattered and screamed at the waves crashing below. Rose had fallen asleep under the umbrella next to Ah Zee, and Jack was still on his towel. Sugar walked over carrying a plate of sausage and pepper sandwiches and a couple of cans of cream soda.

"Don't let your father bother you," she said, nudging her daughter's shoulder with the plate. "Besides, what was that boy doing anyway?"

"Nothing. I fell."

"Well, don't let him upset you. You know how he is."

What is that supposed to mean? It was her mother's answer to everything when it came to her father. She wasn't even sure her mother knew what it meant. Mattina took one of the sandwiches and a soda.

"Here, Ah Zee," Sugar handed a sandwich and a soda to the aunt. "See if your brother wants one of these when he wakes up," she said to Mattina and left the plate on the blanket.

Mattina sat listening to the soda fizz in the can while she watched the juices of her sandwich glisten in the sunlight. She looked down the beach and saw that her cousins were now in the water. The boy with the wire-rimmed sunglasses had Mindy on his shoulders, and the boy with the dog tooth had Cindy on his. Each girl was struggling to knock the other off. The fat pale boy was swimming around them trying to pull the girls down from behind, but no one was paying any attention to him. The boy with the shaggy blonde hair was sitting near the shore watching. Mattina hoped that he'd look up her way.

"Don't let him get to you," Jack said, as he sat down on his sister's blanket and took a sandwich. "He thinks he has to do those things in order to look tough. Next time, just tell him to leave you alone."

"Yeah. Right. How could I tell him that?"

"What's he gonna do? Yell?"

"I can't say that to him. You know how he is," she said, surprised at how easily her mother's words came to her. "Besides, you shouldn't talk. You're here."

Jack shook his head and got up to go back to his towel. "Not for long," he said as he left. Her brother was always saying that he was going to join the army or go to Canada or something. It made her nervous when he talked about leaving because he would be eighteen soon and she knew, eventually, that he would. She pulled his white tee closer as she watched him sitting across from her, his shoulder-length hair tangling in the breeze.

Mattina put her sandwich back on the plate and lay down on her back with her head tilted to the side, so she could see the water. The heat created a wavy distortion as it reflected off the sand. Down the long western shoreline, she watched as the waves crashed into the dark jagged rocks, vapor pinks and purples floated above.

The mid-day sun pressed down on her. She closed her eyes and saw the warm glow breaking through. The heavy rhythm of the ocean rocked her mind as she listened to the prattle of the gulls. She reached down, grabbed a handful of sand, and let it slowly fall through her fingers. She began to feel as though she were floating above everyone. Above Jack and Rose and Ah Zee. Above Sugar and Carmine and Uncle Sal and Aunt Baby. Above the twins and the boys. Half awake, half asleep, rising toward the white hot sun.

The words that penetrated her dream seemed foreign, yet were familiar. Their urgency immediately pulled her back down to the sand. She quickly sat up and looked around for Rose, who was still asleep. It was Ah Zee who was leaning forward in her beach chair. *"Guardi!"* she kept repeating and nodding toward the water.

Mattina looked down the beach and saw that her cousins were still playing with the two boys. Then, she looked beyond and saw that the fat pale boy had swum far past them, and his wide round head was bobbing in and out of the water.

"Hey, you guys!" The boy with the shaggy blonde hair stood up from his spot near the shore and called to his friends. "Look," he shouted as he pointed to the fat pale boy.

The two boys quickly threw the girls off their shoulders and began swimming out to the drowning boy. Uncle Sal, Carmine, and some of the other men also ran into the water and began swimming out to help. Jack stood up and, for the first time, seemed interested in what was going on.

Mattina stood up, too. But she was looking at something else. While the others continued to swim out past the breaking waves to try and save the fat pale boy, Carmine had stopped running and was just standing in the shallow surf, the hems of his trunks dangling inches above the water. *Why isn't he going in?* She wondered and glanced over to Ah Zee, who was calmly watching Carmine.

The two boys finally got to the drowning boy and began to haul him back to shore. Uncle Sal and one of his friends also reached the boy and helped tow him in. Mattina saw that her father had completely backed out of the water and was standing on the shore. Sugar and Aunt Baby ran down and stood a few feet behind him.

"Is he all right?" Aunt Baby called.

"Bring 'em in over here," Carmine said, as he directed the men, who carried the fat pale boy by his arms and legs and dropped him onto the sand.

The group was now gathered around the boy, who was coughing up salt water and catching his breath.

"He must have gotten a cramp," Aunt Baby said.

"Did he just eat?" Sugar asked. "You can't eat and then go in."

"Okay. Okay...Everybody relax. The kid's not dead," Uncle Sal announced after a quick inspection. But the boy with the dog tooth and the boy with the wire-rimmed sunglasses decided to walk the fat pale boy over to the first aid tent on the east side.

"He's fine," Jack said, and returned to his towel, disappointed in the show.

As the excitement died down, some of the women began barbequing again. The men opened a few more beers. Mindy and Cindy finally came up to the tables, ate a couple of hot dogs, spread out a blanket, and worked on their tans. Uncle Sal slid in his new Beatles tape and turned up the volume. Carmine complained about the crazy music.

The sun was inching toward the giant dark rocks to the west. Mattina sat back down on her blanket and watched as the waves continued to crash against them, spraying green and pink misty bars into the sky. She leaned back, slid out of her shorts, took off Jack's white tee, and unbraided her hair. Sitting there in her tight suit, she felt her arms and legs begin to burn.

At first she hesitated, but then got up and walked to the water's edge. The seagulls circled above her arguing among themselves. The foamy surf covered her feet as she slowly sank into the sand. Each time the shallow remains of a wave rushed back into the ocean, she felt as though her entire body was speeding backward toward the land behind her. As a child, the odd sensation had always fascinated her. But now as she observed the watery phenomenon, she could see that it all had been an illusion.

Mattina walked into the icy water and headed toward the dark mysterious rocks. A hazy rainbow of colors appeared above them. As she struggled to get beyond the breakers, she saw that the boy with the shaggy blonde hair was swimming toward her. She dove into an oncoming wave. The water ignited her body, and the salt burned her throat. When she came up for air, she thought she heard someone calling her from the shore. The boy with the shaggy blonde hair also dove into a wave and resurfaced in front of her. His hair was matted back and, for the first time, she could see his little brown eyes. But she didn't stop to look into his eyes. She looked ahead and swam toward the rocky world that waited for her.

ABOUT THE AUTHORS

Ness Boers has published many fan fiction pieces. *The Boy With a Thousand Arms i*s her first published piece of literary fiction.

Katie Burns is a 28 year old student and lives in Albany, N.Y.

Colleen Maloney resides in a quiet bit of green in the shadow of an old mountain with her husband, children and various critters. She has a Bachelor of Arts focusing in English and Anthropology coupled with a passion for all things ancient. When not writing she can usually be found in the garden desperately trying to change the color of her thumbs.

J S McInroy is a wholly imaginary person with 999 arms.

Maria Palmara teaches literature and creative writing at a community college in Upstate New York. Her dissertation includes a collection of short stories entitled *More Like Me Than Myself.*

Edward K. Ryan is a lifelong resident of upstate New York. He is the author of one novel, *Thinner Than Blood,* and is currently working on his second. He writes in the spaces around life as a husband and father.

William Schultz is a freelance writer living in New York's capital region. He considers himself strange and unfathomable, but the people at Slate Run Publishing make him seem downright normal by comparison.

Ryan Smithson served in the Army Corps of Engineers in Iraq from 2004-2005. Upon returning home, he began writing about his experiences for a college English class. His writing eventually culminated in his memoir, *Ghosts of War: The True Story of a 19-Year-Old GI*, published by HarperCollins in 2009. He lives in Rotterdam, NY with his wife and two children.

James J. Slattery is the author of the novel *Army Girl* and is currently working on his next book which he hopes to publish in the summer of 2015. He is also the author of the personal chronicle *DIE LIVE LOVE*. He lives in North Greenbush, NY and is an adjunct instructor at Hudson Valley Community College.

Stephen Slattery is the author of the novel *Barrooms*. He was born in Wellsboro, Pennsylvania and raised in Berlin, New York. For many years he worked as a supervisor in New England residential treatment facilities. Today he lives in Western Massachusetts with his wife and children.

Mr. Slattery can be contacted on Facebook or at swslattery@yahoo.com.

Also available from Slate Run Publishing, LLC

In trade paperback and electronic forms:

www.ingramcontent.com/pod-product-compliance
Lightning Source LLC
Chambersburg PA
CBHW021035130626
46552CB00005B/1858